BETTER WITH YOU

SIMON & AYLIN

THE KERRIGAN FAMILY
BOOK 1

ANDREA FINNELLY

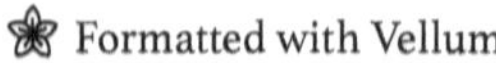 Formatted with Vellum

PROLOGUE

Simon Kerrigan stared out the window of his apartment at the family resort, the sky blackened by night, soft lights around Lake Tola making the water glisten slightly with the waves. A storm blew in, the rare winter lightning in the distance illuminated the night sky. It was perfect for the mood he was in.

His mother was dead.

Two weeks later, he slumped on his couch, glass in hand full of the top shelf whiskey he kept in the decanter. He didn't even remember getting it. Simon wondered how many times he needed to remind himself that his mother was dead before his brain believed it. He thought it had been plenty of time.

He had finally felt as though he wasn't working on autopilot anymore. It wasn't easy, but being at work gave him something to occupy his mind. Paperwork was the hardest to concentrate on and he'd admit that was not getting done up to his standards right now.

Being around the staff was still hard. They'd loved her, too.

But the guests at Cypress Bay Manor Resort were what really kept him occupied. He'd immersed himself in customer relations in the last week, and it had been easier to laugh and converse with the guests than it had the week before.

His mother's death was such a shock to everyone, not just those who worked at the resort. Lauren Kerrigan had her hand in all kinds of projects and committees all over town. And the way she died was even more heartbreaking for them all. She had so much life at only fifty-one and now she was gone.

The entire family had spent a wonderful three weeks with his maternal grandparents, who were visiting from England for Christmas and New Year's.

His mother and her parents had moved to the States for her father's job when she was in high school. When she graduated, his grandparents decided they missed England, moving back after she married his father John. They frequently came to visit —more so when Simon and his brother Oliver were kids—but they were close with his mother and visited a couple of times a year.

When it was time for them to leave, his mother drove them to the airport in Orlando. Something she did every time they came to visit. No one thought anything of it. His mother often handled the drive without any problems. Even at night, as it was by the time she made her way home. But she never made it.

Simon shuddered at the memory of the day they lost her.

"Simon, have you heard anything from your mother?" his father asked.

"Why would I?" he responded. He didn't have time for this. He was already behind work because of the holidays and his grandparents' visit. And he was tired. So tired with all the paperwork that was piled up on his desk. He shouldn't have taken all those days off.

"She should be home by now and I haven't heard from her," his father John said, a slight tinge of panic in his voice.

"You know Mum and how much she hates using the hands free device in her car. She probably ran into some traffic."

"Right. You're right. I'll talk to you later," John said despondently.

His father hung up the phone and Simon got back to work, immediately forgetting all about the call and his parents. He was so involved with his work that Simon almost didn't realize the phone was ringing again an hour later.

"Yeah, this is Simon," he answered impatiently.

"Your mother was in an accident," his father said. This perked Simon up and lifted his attention away from his work.

"Is she alright? Does she need someone to come pick her up?" he asked. "I can leave now and drive to wherever she is to get her."

"No, there's no need for it. She's gone. Simon she's gone. They killed her," his father whispered, tears choking as he tried to talk.

"What?" Simon sat in his office, stunned. Gone? His Mum was dead? How could that be? He'd spoken with her that morning before he went back to work. He didn't even get the chance to say goodbye when she left with his grandparents for the airport.

Simon shook off the memory. They later found out a wrong way driver had hit her head on, killing her instantly. It was worse to learn that the man who was driving drunk only received minor injuries. He wasn't even supposed to be driving, his license revoked because of repeated incidents of driving under the influence. Now he was being charged with manslaughter, though Simon couldn't bring himself to care what happened to him. It wouldn't bring his mother back.

Now here it was, in the middle of the night, two weeks later, and he was still trying to come to terms with it all. Simon would never forgive himself for the way he blew off his father the first time he called. Or how he didn't get to say goodbye to his mother before she left for what would be the last time he would see her.

Lauren Kerrigan was the life of the family. A mere five foot two inches with a big personality and plenty of sass. She taught her boys the 'proper' way to speak, using words like cheeky, gobsmacked, and wonky. Those went over really well at school.

His friends loved it, his teachers not so much. He often saved his British colloquialisms and slang for family, though they sometimes popped out when he was tired, angry, or not thinking about what was coming out of his mouth.

He heaved out an enormous sigh. Maybe going back to work would help. It was all he seemed to do these days. Of course, it wasn't as if he didn't work too much before. He was currently in charge of the family resort—so much so that he lived on the property in the private family quarters—and always considered himself to be on call.

Glancing down at his glass, Simon determined he didn't have too much to drink. Barely a sip at all. Setting down the glass, he walked out the door, letting it lock behind him.

He would check with the night crew first, make sure they had everything under control, then go to his office to finish up some of that bloody paperwork. He hated all the paperwork. And at the same time, it did keep him busy. Even if he'd rather be doing anything else at the resort.

Walking through the corridor to the employees' only door and out into the lobby, Simon walked with purpose through the lounge toward the front desk. He always loved walking through the resort. It gave him a sense of pride that his family made it, and here he was, years later, carrying on their work and legacy. It also had his mother's sense of savvy design all over it, which made him both sad and comforted.

Approaching the front desk, he witnessed the night clerk, Tiffany, talking to a decidedly frazzled family of four. Simon arrived in time to catch the end of their conversation.

"Thank you so much! I'm not sure what we would have done if you didn't have a room available," said the father of two young and—to Simon's eye—unusually well-behaved boys.

"You're very welcome, sir," Tiffany told the man. "Here are your keys. You'll find the elevator down this hallway and to your right. Your room is a family suite, located on the second floor."

The man thanked her again before gathering their luggage and walking toward the elevators.

"Any problems, Tiffany?" he asked.

"No. It's lucky for them that this is the off season and we have a room. Said they traveled from Michigan to go to the parks, but decided at the last minute they didn't want to stay in the city. They wanted to give their boys a less 'metropolitan' vacation — his words, not mine," she said with a chuckle.

Simon gave a small smile that didn't quite reach his eyes. "Well, I hope they enjoy themselves. Not as much to do in January here. Lake Tola Beach isn't even open for swimming, though I suppose they can take a blustery boat tour with Joel."

"What do you want to bet they check out in a day or two and head back down to Orlando?" she asked.

"We can probably count on it," he said.

Simon said his goodbye's to the desk clerk and made his way down the hallway behind the front desk to his office. He unlocked and opened the door, looking around as though seeing it for the first time.

Bookshelves in a deep mahogany lined the back wall, filled with books and trinkets his paternal grandparents, parents and he added from various sources and travels. Awards for the resort adorned a glass-doored cabinet on the other side of the room. They frequently had the newest awards and other recognition given out in the lobby. This held past accolades, of which there were many thanks to the work his family put into the resort over the generations.

In the corner sat a small table with a couple of chairs for impromptu meetings or a meal. He admitted he enjoyed drinking his tea during the midday break. He even had a small cart with an electric teakettle and a couple jars of loose leaf tea, courtesy of his cousin Hailee.

And finally, in the center of the room sat his desk—again mahogany to match the bookshelves—disheveled with stacks of papers, pens, and other office supplies surrounding the spot where he kept his laptop. A comfortable office chair sat behind the desk and two other chairs positioned in front of it.

Simon sat down in his chair and thought about the family who had just come into the Cypress Bay Manor Resort.

He always wanted a family of his own, someone to spend his life with and watch their children grow into adults together.

With his mother's death, he had an idea of how it felt to have someone he loved so deeply in his life, only to lose them. He wasn't so sure he was willing to go through that again.

It hurt that it was his mother who died—it should have been the eejit who hit her. Eejit. Though the word for idiot was more Irish than British, his mother loved that word and used it often both as an insult and a term of affection. It left a big hole in his heart, remembering.

But seeing what his father was going through, the deep and never-ending grief. Simon was grieving, too, but it couldn't compare to the pain his father was going through. His father lost the love of his life, someone who he expected to grow old with, spending every moment together after they'd done their job of raising Simon and his brother.

Simon couldn't imagine living his entire life without the love and joy of having his own family. It was all he had ever dreamed about. At thirty-two, he was ready for the wife and family. Yet he didn't want to risk losing her once he found her, either. It conflicted him. He had hoped that someday it would be his children who ran the resort. Now he wasn't entirely sure if he cared about that anymore.

And even with that, Simon still had work to do. The resort would only run itself for so long without him managing it. Not that he thought he was the only one who could run the resort, but he was the one currently in charge and so it fell on him to carry on. And wasn't that so British.

His mother would be so proud.

1

About five months later.

"Why did you need to go to Florida to finish your book?"

Aylin Miller relaxed in her cabin, sinking into the couch while talking on the phone to her friend and editor, Angeline. Getting away made her feel safe again. Her whole body sighed in relief once the tension she had been gripping in it had eased away. It was like all the worries of the last few months were suddenly wiped away.

"You know why I needed to leave. And coming to Florida was your idea, remember?"

"Of course, I know why you left. By why so far away? What was I thinking when I said Florida? It's so hot you're going to melt!"

Aylin laughed, "They do have air conditioning, you know."

"Yeah, but you'll need to go out sometime."

Not if she could help it, Aylin thought. She had to finish her book. After everything she'd been through these past several months, she was ready for some peace and quiet, with no disruptions—or someone stalking her. The stillness in the cabin gave her exactly what she needed.

Finishing up her conversation with Angeline, Aylin studied the cabin, picturing herself in the space for the summer. The cabin was simple, no frills. Its two-room layout meant fewer distractions, not that she was easily distracted.

Once she got into the zone, it was hard for her to escape it. All she needed was an area to work. Of course, it also meant she frequently forgot to stop for food. That could be a problem. She reminded herself to call over to the resort to have her meals delivered to the cabin.

The main room contained a galley kitchen on one side of the room, a small round table with two chairs under one of the front windows, and an island with two stools. It separated the kitchen from the living room area, which held a loveseat couch and two comfortable looking chairs positioned around a coffee table.

The space for the television was empty because Angeline asked them to remove it when she made the reservations for the cabin. She knew Aylin well. The view would be enough for her as it was—she didn't need the constant droning from late night programming ruining her schedule.

As for the view, the cabin had a sliding glass door across from the front door that almost took up the entire wall and could be opened completely. Once open, it left an incredible view of the woods and lake, as well as access to the square patio. It was like living in a forest, the glistening of the sun bouncing off the water, like diamonds sparkling, cutting right through the slight foliage. A path led to the lake, the small sliver of beach seemed like a great place to lie around, if she was into that sort of thing.

Turning toward the other room, she walked into the cabin's bedroom. Aylin needed to finish unpacking if she wanted to set up her work area and get back into her book. The bedroom was sparse, but well decorated. The king-sized bed took up most of the room, facing a set of windows with that fabulous view again. With the two suitcases and computer bag she brought with her spread over it, the sage green bedspread barely seen beneath them.

On the other wall sat an armoire, where she started putting her clothes before she remembered to call Angeline. Of course, she only hung up a couple of shirts, so her suitcases remained unpacked. Tucked into the corner was the desk and chair she requested. It was small, but she only needed enough room for her laptop. And maybe some of her office supplies, the portable printer she managed to cram inside one of her suitcases, and the books she used for reference.

Finally, a door next to the bed led into the bathroom. Again...not much there, a basic toilet, sink and shower, done in a lovely creamy peach color. White towels stacked on the open wall shelves, along with a variety of supplies, soaps, toilet paper, and other bottles she would inspect later. Overall, the cabin was clean, nicely decorated, and well-suited to her needs.

"That's enough time wasting," she told herself out loud. "It's time to unpack and finish setting up the desk. How else am I supposed to work?"

Shaking her head, Aylin finished putting her clothes away in the armoire. Haphazardly hanging her shirts, thinking she should probably iron them, but knew she wouldn't. From her luggage, she pulled the stacks of jeans, undergarments, and socks and placed them in the open drawers.

The toiletry bag was the last item she pulled from her suitcase. Aylin dumped it on the bathroom counter, then walked back into the bedroom to take care of the empty suitcases. She closed them up and shoved them under the bed so she wouldn't trip over them.

The computer bag came next. Aylin grabbed it and walked over to the desk to set up her workspace. Placing the bag on the chair, she opened it to remove a laptop, which she carefully set on top of the desk. It should have been set up first to charge, but what was done was done, she thought as she plugged it in.

Aylin continued to pull out what she considered her tools of the trade. An external hard drive, a handful of flash drives — she could never have too many backups — notebooks of various sizes and pens to jot down ideas, and two piles of index cards bound by rubber bands.

Letting out a big breath, her shoulders drooped at the thought of not having her board with her. It was too big to fit into her bags, so she had to leave it at home. The board was a forty-eight by thirty-six inch bulletin board where she put up her index cards. Seeing all her cards in some semblance of order in front of her helped keep her on track when writing her books. She should have bought the one that folded in threes instead.

Maybe the hotel had something? If not, she'd just look around town. Or...eyeing the walls around the desk, Aylin thought she may be able to tape her cards to the walls. Damn... now she needed tape.

With her desk in order and everything in its place for her to begin, the last thing Aylin felt like doing was sitting after her long flight from Philadelphia.

A three-hour layover in D.C. before catching the plane to Orlando made her cranky. If it wasn't for the last minute plans, she would have found a direct flight. She was lucky to find one at the last-minute. All the direct flights were booked, and she found the only flight with one layover stop.

But again, what was done was done, and she wasn't going to let it bother her.

It was probably why she was cranky. All she wanted to do was whine, flop down onto the bed, and take a nap.

The airports were crowded, and she hated crowds. It was one of the many reasons why she loved her job. She stayed in her apartment—or cabin, in this case—and wrote without having many people around her. Unless she chose to be around a lot of people.

That this cabin was even available for the whole summer was even more lucky. Tourist areas in Florida were usually booked months in advance—especially those that were this close to Orlando. Apparently, the resort recently completed the finishing touches on remodeling this cabin and had not booked it yet when Angeline called to set it up for her.

Even with a lot of tourists around, she would be able to concentrate on her work. Living and working in Philadelphia, she often got so into her work that the background noise of the city fell away. Occasionally, way too much traffic or other chaos going on made it hard to block it out.

Here, she wouldn't even need to worry about that. It was so quiet the wind blowing through the trees made soft, whooshing sounds as they moved against each other. If she was the type to pay attention to it.

At this point, Aylin would be happy with anywhere as long as it was away from where she was. She loved her city and apartment, but after what happened, she needed to leave. Shaking herself out of her thoughts, she decided to get out of the cabin and find out if the resort had a board or at least some tape she could borrow.

Stepping out of her cabin, Aylin locked the door and headed down the path toward the main resort building, which the resort called Cypress Manor—a shortened version of the whole resort name of Cypress Bay Manor Resort. It was a mouthful, so she understood why they shortened it when referring to the main building.

There was a cabin on her right with a couple leaving with their luggage. It looked like she would get a new neighbor soon. Hope whomever took over the cabin was too busy with their own vacation to bother her. On her left, a man was entering the third cabin the resort had available. He turned his head, staring at her before closing the door. Aylin shivered. Well, that was creepy, she thought and continued on her way.

Entering Cypress Manor's lobby, she asked the desk clerk if she had what Aylin needed. They didn't have exactly what she wanted, but she was able to come away with some tape. It would do for now. She may want to check in town for a store with something better later on.

Satisfied she had done what she set out to do, Aylin decided she still didn't want to go back to her cabin yet. She needed to shake off this restlessness before writing. Besides, it was so nice outside. Well, it wasn't exactly nice. It was hotter than anything she was used to, but the breeze coming off the lake helped take it down a notch and the shade during her walk from the cabin made it tolerable.

She would walk around the resort grounds, checking out the beach and lake, then walk back through the woods to her cabin. Wandering always helped her flesh out ideas and who knew what would happen at a resort by the lake in her mind.

On her way down the path surrounded by manicured lawns, she passed by a fenced in pool area and eatery before coming to the lake. Facing Lake Tola, her back to the resort, Aylin glanced to her right. There was a dock with a pontoon boat tied to it, Madris Boat and Lake Tours lettered boldly in a bright blue on the side. Next to the dock was a dock house, huge barn-like doors opened in the middle of the building, where she assumed people would go to get information and schedule a boat tour.

Turning her head in the other direction, she spotted a long pier with a covered gazebo at the end that was sitting over the lake. That could be a good thinking spot. A person would feel like she was in the middle of the water, standing at the end. Though the people that were walking up and down the pier and hanging out in the gazebo may dissuade her from attempting it.

Further down the beach, Aylin noticed a man standing off by himself. He was tall...six feet at least, if not more. He was taller than her measly five foot six, that was for sure. By her estimation, she would barely come up to his shoulders, which would suit her just fine.

He had his light brown hair styled back off a face that had a sharp, angled profile. She made out some scruff around his jawline and chin. Aylin imagined what it would be like to feel that scruff on the palm of her hand as she caressed his face. He looked so lost in thought that she wondered what would happen if she went over to him and gave him a hug.

The man suddenly shook his head, as if trying to thwart some wayward thought. Turning away from the water, he walked back toward the resort without checking out his surroundings. He was probably someone who was used to the beach, lake, and all the people. So much so, he didn't even notice them anymore; she thought.

Girl, what are you doing? Aylin chastised herself for thinking about the man. This is not the time to get involved with anyone. Her only goals for this trip were to finish her book and figure out how she could safely go back home.

And that was it! No time for romance.

She couldn't let anyone else get involved in what was going on. It was bad enough that she had her friend and parents worried about her, though her parents thought she should let the police deal with it and continue with her life as usual. They didn't understand why she had to leave Philadelphia for a while. Not that she told them everything.

Priorities firmly back in place, Aylin quick marched back toward her cabin. It was time to get back to work!

2

At the edge of the lake, Simon reflected on the last few months. He needed this time away from the resort for a little while, where no one would find him. Not that he was hiding or anything. He was still standing out in the open, but most wouldn't think to look for him on the beach. Unless he was with his family, it wasn't something he normally did, especially in the middle of a workday.

He only needed a moment to decompress before getting back to work.

His father was driving him crazy in the time since his mother was killed. His father's intense grief started easing up a little about three months in, not that his father had stopped grieving altogether. He lost a piece of himself when Simon's mother died. But it was lessened enough to have him wanting to be more involved. The man was becoming impossible to deal with.

This was supposed to be his semi-retirement. Instead, John Kerrigan, Jr., decided he needed to be involved in everything at the resort, inserting himself into projects that were already firmly in the works. He was disrupting their employees and making a commotion they couldn't have with all the tourists staying with them right now.

Simon knew it was only a matter of time before his father tried to worm his way into other areas of the resort. All he needed was for his father to try to take over his job or his brother Oliver's, who was a chef and managed the kitchen and food services at the resort. He couldn't let him carry on like this. Simon had been running interference all week, trying to redirect his father so their employees could work.

How was he supposed to manage his own grief, the resort, and his father on his own? Oliver should step up with their father, too. Simon knew his brother was also grieving, not that anyone would notice.

They always teased Oliver that he kept a stiff upper lip, as his mother would say, showing no emotion, but he understood his brother well. While Oliver kept everything internalized, he could only hold it in for so long. Simon was just waiting for the day when he'd blow. All that intense emotion would come tumbling out at once and for anyone in his vicinity...watch out!

He remembered as a child it would come out in the form of breaking or throwing toys. As a teenager, he would get into fights. As an adult, Oliver so far had been pretty good at keeping a lid on, but Simon really didn't want to see what would happen with all the grief he was holding in.

Perhaps he should talk to his uncles and have them run interference with his father. His father had three surviving brothers. Add in their wives and kids—his aunts and cousins—and there sure were enough of them to handle his father. They were his family, too, damn it! Why shouldn't they be involved?

Giving an internal sigh, Simon knew why they would not interfere. This was resort business now. Each one would support his father outside of work, but they all turned over their shares of the resort over to their children. It was their turn to handle any problems that arose. Including John Kerrigan,

Jr.'s grief induced need to insinuate himself into everything at the resort.

Simon took one last look at the lake, thinking how lucky he was to live in a place so beautiful and relaxing. Now if only he could have some of that beauty and relaxation in his life all the time. Yeah, like he would ever relax. He had a business he ran practically twenty-four seven. He even lived at the resort, so the staff figured he was available and always on call. At any moment, his free time could be disrupted.

And as for beauty. Well, it was around him every day. The resort, the lake, the beauty of them were all around him on a daily basis. But he wanted more than that. Simon wanted to share in the beauty of what was around him with a wife and family. Or he did. Maybe. He wasn't sure what he wanted anymore.

Loving, then losing someone you loved was hell!

They had lost his paternal grandparents, John Sr. and Marinda Kerrigan, a few months into the pandemic, victims of the early wave of COVID-19. His grandmother fell ill first, his grandfather followed soon after—almost as though he couldn't bear to live without her. Their deaths were a heavy blow to the family, a tragic end to the lives of two people who had poured everything into building the resort from the ground up. But their legacy lived on, carried forward first by his father, and then Simon with help from the rest of the Kerrigans.

Add in the sudden loss of his mother almost six months ago, and it was just too much for him to manage.

Perhaps someday he'd find what he was looking for, though he wasn't sure how it would happen if he never left the resort. Thinking of the resort, he realized how long he had been gone. He really did need to return. Who knew what his father was getting into now!

Simon shook his head at that thought, turned without looking around. Walking back toward the resort to continue the rest of his day, he examined the building in front of him as he trudged up the small hill to where it stood.

The Cypress Bay Manor Resort had been in the Kerrigan family since his paternal grandparents, John and Marinda Kerrigan, bought the old dilapidated building and renovated it with help from the town. They put in a lot of hard work to change the building from its plain exterior to one with a slightly Victorian-like flair, painted in a soft yellow. A wide wrap-around porch and added decorative trim around the windows and doors were painted in a creamy white.

The interior was also immaculately designed and decorated. When guests first walked in, they entered the lobby and lounge area, one open room decorated in creams and a muted soft green. The many front windows lit up the room during the day when the sun came through them. The wood floor warmed the space, keeping it from becoming washed out.

Comfortable chairs and sofas flanked two fireplaces at either end of the room, encouraging guests to sit, mingle, and relax. The lobby's front desk was built into the wall, giving it a seamless look so it didn't detract from the overall decor of the room. Carpeted stairs on the left of the front desk brought guests to the upper floors. While going right led to the entrance to the offices, a commercial kitchen to accommodate all their eateries, and his private living quarters.

Beyond the stairs, a hallway led to the elevators, restrooms, a restaurant they named Tola Dining after the lake, conference, and event rooms, a fitness center. A tavern added by his parents called BritSip Tavern, frequently known as 'The Tavern', was also on that side of the main building.

The commercial kitchen was set up in a zone-style layout. It not only provided food for Tola Dining but also for BritSip Tavern and the poolside eatery known as The Basin. Occasionally, they would be tasked with providing food for larger events that took place at the resort, though often they would request those events to be catered by other companies. Those catering companies would still need a place to set up, and so they had a space for them in the kitchen as well.

The second and third floors had varying types of guest rooms. Five guest rooms with either a single king bed or two queen beds were located on the second floor, all with their own bathrooms. The second floor also had two family suites on either end of the hallway, which each had a king bed and two twin beds in slightly larger rooms, also with their own bathrooms.

The third floor was where their suites were located. Three two-bedroom suites, each with their own bathrooms and parlors, occupied the entire third floor. Each suite had windows that gave their guests a view of both the lake from one side and the historic town on the other side.

When his father took over the resort, he added the cabins near the wooded side of the resort. The three cabins all had a peaceful quality to them that let their guests have privacy and yet still had easy access to the main resort building. The cabins all had a lake view and a wooded view, but were not easily visible from Cypress Manor or the beach area. Simon was planning to add more cabins, but was still working on the plans and where exactly to put them, so it didn't appear too crowded in the woods surrounding the resort.

His parents also renamed the main building of the resort into simply 'Cypress Manor'. It was yet another nod to his British mother. As if the entire name of the resort wasn't posh enough. Cypress Bay Manor Resort already sounded as though it belonged in an English countryside rather than next to a lake in the middle of Florida. But since that was a mouthful, Cypress Manor was born.

Now all the Kerrigan cousins owned a piece of the resort, though not all wanted to work the resort as their primary job.

Simon was proud and privileged to be the one who managed it as the resort's CEO.

His brother Oliver was a chef. He managed the kitchen and everything food related—the kitchen, dining room, tavern, and poolside eatery. His cousin Marinda was in charge of customer relations and coordinated the staff for the hotel. Her sister Ryleigh was in maintenance. She split her time between her own jobs around Cypress Bay and the resort, working on maintenance issues or building something for them as needed.

The remaining cousins had jobs of their own. Katia owned a sandwich and deli shop. Hailee owned a book and tea shop. Luke was the county sheriff, while his twin brother was a doctor. Noah spent a lot of his time at the hospital in Pine Grove—the town directly to their north—and some working with Dr. Mancera at the clinic in downtown Cypress Bay. When he wasn't busy with either of those, he was often found hanging around Luke or relaxing in his apartment.

Climbing the wide steps that led to the veranda, Simon gave a smile. Every time he entered the building, he felt his family close by and wasn't that what life should be all about?

If only they were all still around to enjoy each other and the resort they built together.

3

Two days later and Aylin was finally deep into her writing. The first day she spent getting her index cards organized on the wall in front of the desk. It made her miss the board at home, where she would pin her cards up and move them around easily. Tape was all she had, so she would make it work.

Taping them on the wall wasn't too bad, and she could still look up to immediately see where she should go in her story. Though it was a pain when she needed to reposition a card around.

Now where did she put that damn tape?

Yesterday was the first day where she was able to do any real writing. Just being able to get the words out made her feel like she was finally accomplishing something.

Still, the deadline she set for herself was looming and she was horribly behind on it. It wasn't like she was going to be in trouble with her publisher. At this point, she had built up enough of a reputation that they knew she would complete what they wanted on time.

The deadline was one of her own making and something

she always put in place to make sure she had time for all the other things she needed to do. Writing wasn't the only thing she had to do as an author. She also had to make revisions after it came back from her editor—sometimes more than once—and do all the marketing. That meant getting her monthly newsletter out and having actual conversations with her fans, among other things.

Despite being behind her deadline, the words were coming fast for her today. It would not always be this way, so she would take advantage of it. She just may catch up at this rate. Focusing on her book, she brainstormed.

The kid had a hard life, but it shaped him into the hard young man he was today. He went from running drugs for his parents to being the top dealer in the tri-state area.

What her hero would do when he encountered the drug dealer kingpin in the warehouse after the intense investigation?

Was he still a loose cannon after losing his wife? After all, the very people he was chasing blew her up. It should have been prevented, but he made a very critical mistake, leading to his wife's unfortunate death right in front of him.

He wasn't as careful as he should have been in his investigations. He got too close, and they made him...

Aylin was so involved in her work that the sound of a heavy bang at her front door startled her. It threw her off her writing stride, making her jump in her seat. Taking a deep breath, she figured it was probably only the person delivering her room service. Did she actually order room service yet today? Aylin couldn't remember if that was today or yesterday.

Whenever it was, someone was clearly at the door now. Aylin decided she might as well take a break. Her momentum was already interrupted and if she didn't stop to eat, then she would most likely forget all together.

Walking to the door, Aylin opened it, expecting someone

from Tola Dining standing there with a tray, their golf cart parked in front of the cabin. Instead, she was shocked to see a potted plant in pieces on the front stoop. The ceramic blue pot was in broken shards, dirt in a heap and spread all over. The plant was no longer in the safety of its pot and dirt appeared to be intact. Turning slightly, she examined the door and noticed a dent in it with flecks of dirt covering the area where it hit.

Looking around, she didn't see anyone in the area who could have done this. Why would anyone throw a potted plant at her door? It made little sense to her.

Could this be related to what happened to her at home? How could it, though? No one knew she was in Cypress Bay other than Angeline. She didn't even tell her parents exactly where she was going, for cripes' sake!

Aylin thought back to what had happened at home before she left for Florida. She was out for the day, meeting Angeline for lunch and planning a night out to celebrate once her latest book was complete. When she got home, a police officer was standing in front of her apartment door.

"Hello, officer. Umm...this is my apartment. What's going on?"

"Ma'am, can I please see some identification?"

Aylin looked at him warily, but took out her wallet and handed him her identification. The officer scanned it and then handed it back.

"Ms. Miller, there was a break-in at your apartment. A neighbor heard a disturbance and called it in. When we got here, the door was open, and it looked as though someone was going through your apartment."

Aylin stood there in shock. Someone broke into her apartment. Her computer! All her work! She quickly stepped forward, wanting to go into her apartment to make sure her work area was still intact. The officer stopped her from going toward the door by blocking it, putting his hands up in a placating manner.

"I'm sorry, Ms. Miller, but you'll need to stay out here until the officers finish processing your apartment."

"I need to make sure my work is okay. Was anything taken? Did you catch the person who did this?"

"We'll take you through your apartment in a moment so you can let us know if anything is missing. The person got away, but the woman across the hall said she got a look at a man leaving your apartment."

"Good. So she can identify him as soon as you find him."

"Unfortunately, she can't identify him and her description won't help us find him. She said he was a short man wearing all black, a big bulky jacket, scarf around his face, and a ball cap with the bill pulled down. She said she was afraid to be seen, so she was looking through the peephole."

"Well, damn it. That could be anyone, then." Aylin was frustrated that she couldn't go into her apartment. She really needed to get inside to see it for herself.

Just then, another officer stepped out of her apartment. The officer in front of the door gestured to her and told him Aylin was the resident.

"You can go on in, Ms. Miller. We'll need you to tell us if anything is missing," the other officer said. "Keep in mind, the apartment is a mess and the person who broke in spray painted something on your living room wall."

She carefully stepped inside and could barely figure out what she was actually seeing. Her apartment was a mess, like the officer told her. Her bookshelf and books were strewn all over the living room, as were the dishes from her kitchen. But what shocked her the most was the bold orange writing on her living room wall:

You will die for what you have done

Aylin shivered just thinking about the scene, even though it happened weeks ago. Thankfully, whoever broke into her apartment only managed to destroy her living room and kitchen before being scared off. He never got the chance to make it into the back rooms, including her writing space.

This incident with the pot couldn't be related to what happened at home in Philadelphia. But obviously some angry person thought whoever they didn't like was inside this cabin. Or there could be a gang of kids wandering around with nothing better to do than throw potted plants at cabin doors.

She could not work this way and needed a quiet place to finish her book. Aylin would go over to Cypress Manor to let them know. Going back inside to grab the key to lock the door, she walked through the woods toward the main resort building.

Entering the resort, Aylin noticed a woman at the front desk and walked directly up to the counter. The nametag pinned to her shirt said Tiffany.

"Good afternoon, Ms. Miller. How can I help you?" Tiffany asked.

"Someone threw a potted plant at my cabin door. I was getting really deep into my work and then Bam!" she said, slapping her hands together. "I came here to have a quiet place to finish my book and thought a cabin in the woods by a lake would be the perfect quiet spot. But now I have pottery being lobbed at my front door, interrupting my flow!"

Aylin stopped when she realized she was yelling and angrier than she thought about the interruption. Tiffany's eyes widened in shock, her mouth hung open for a moment before collecting herself once more. Aylin didn't know if it was because of what she said or because she was yelling at this poor woman who did nothing wrong. Apparently, things like this just didn't happen at the resort.

"I'm so sorr—" she began.

"Mr. Kerrigan, there seems to be an issue with Ms. Miller's cabin," Tiffany calmly interrupted, looking just over Aylin's shoulder. At the woman's words, she turned a little to her right and recognized the man standing next to the front desk for the first time.

Oh, great! Could this get any worse?

First, she started yelling at the front desk clerk and now there was some manager staring at her like she had lost her mind. Discreetly glancing around the lobby, she realized it could get worse. The area held couples, families, and individuals. And they were all staring at her.

"Ms. Miller, why don't we go to my office so we can discuss this further in private," the manager said.

Aylin nodded, staring at the man Tiffany said was Mr. Kerrigan. She suddenly realized this was the same man down on the beach on her first day at the resort. He was a good-looking man from far away. Up close, he was handsome in a rugged, yet clean cut kind of way.

His brown hair was closely cut in what she always thought as a business cut — neatly trimmed all around and styled neatly on top. Scruff covered his jaw, around his mouth, which she noticed pressed together in a frown. His chin pointed slightly at the tip, a dimple only a bit off center, making it asymmetrical.

"Ms. Miller."

"Huh? Oh yeah. Sorry."

Get your head out of the clouds, Aylin! You don't have time to ogle the hot resort manager. You're here for one reason only —to write your book.

Aylin followed the manager around the corner, down a hallway to his office. The office was what she would consider typical, though roomier than she expected. She thought he'd have a closet-sized room that barely fit a desk. Instead, it held a solid wood desk with a comfortable-looking chair behind it. Two more chairs, not as comfortable, she thought as she sat down in front of the desk. There were also lots of awards and bookshelves on various walls around the room.

"Now Ms. Miller..." the man started as he sat down behind the desk.

"Aylin," she corrected.

"Aylin," he conceded. "Would you care to explain what is going on without yelling down the whole resort?"

4

When Simon first turned the corner and saw Aylin Miller standing at the front desk, he was intrigued. Walking over to her, he stared at the woman as she finished up her tirade before she noticed he was standing there.

His initial impression of her was one of interest. Here was a beautiful woman who had no idea she was making a scene in the lobby of his resort. The woman was so fixated on getting her point across that she didn't notice anyone else around her. Tiffany felt the brunt of it although and, seeing him walking out of the hallway from his office, gave a slight nod of her head toward the woman, asking him to come over.

Once Aylin became aware of him, she spent some of her own time staring back at him in return. Not that he minded. She could stare at him all she wanted. It made her all the more intriguing. He had wondered what her explanation would be for yelling at his front desk clerk. And how he could entice her into his bed.

Now that they were in his office, he observed how beautiful she was up close. Oh, there were imperfections and she wasn't what society deemed classically beautiful. But her features just fit together, making a perfectly beautiful picture—to him, anyway. Long straight auburn hair, a face softly rounded with creamy porcelain skin, a small scar running through the corner of her lower lip. He briefly wondered how she got it.

Aylin was on the shorter side and more rounded in her body than most would think was acceptable. All he could think about was how it would feel to hold her close to his own body. Would she soften against all his hardness? He shifted in his seat, wanting to palm himself and move that hardness somewhere more comfortable. Unfortunately, he didn't think he'd ever be comfortable as long as she was in front of him.

Then there were her eyes. The more he stared into them, the more mesmerized he became. Blue as bright as a sapphire. They turned a deeper shade when she was angry, like she was at the front desk. Now that she had calmed down and was a little more on the embarrassed side, the blue calmed, too. Like the clear blue glass of the lake just outside the resort.

Mesmerizing.

If only he was still looking for someone to spend his life with, then Aylin just might be perfect for him. Despite asking her to talk to him calmly, Simon actually liked that she let loose in his resort. It was a refreshing reprieve from the properly put together women he usually took to bed. From what he had seen so far, there would never be a dull moment with her.

Then again, he really didn't know her. Far from it. She was a writer, that much he knew. In the few days she had spent with them, most of her time had her secluded in the cabin.

He made it a point to know some details about all the guests so he and his staff could provide a better experience during their stay. She often forgot to order food to be delivered to her cabin, calling at all hours to set it up. Most likely when she resurfaced and remembered she was hungry. He would need to make sure meals were delivered to her at a set time from now on. She apparently couldn't manage it on her own.

Other than wanting to take care of her—for the sake of her stay, of course—Simon desperately wanted her in his bed. He wasn't looking for someone to spend his life with anymore. He wasn't. And he would keep on telling himself that lie over and over until he started believing it.

Peering at Aylin, he waited for her to answer his question, while wondering what he could do to rile her up again.

"Well, Mr. Kerrigan, I may have gotten a little carried away, but I came here for a quiet place to finish my book. I don't believe it's too much to ask for in a cabin in the middle of nowhere," she accused.

"Yes, that's right. You're an author," he said flippantly.

"You don't have to say author like that."

"Like what exactly?" he asked, amused at her tone.

"Like you just got a whiff of something rotten," she said.

"I can assure you I'm not thinking of any bloody such thing. Now what happened to bring you to my resort in a tiff?" Simon said, knowing it would rile Aylin up. He was really enjoying verbally sparring with her.

"Tiff! Tiff! First, Mr. Kerrigan, who the hell uses a phrase like 'in a tiff' anymore? And second, that's just insulting. Not only to me, but to the desk clerk, Tiffany."

Simon laughed and admitted to himself it could be insulting, but he could not seem to help himself from teasing and saying things that would send Aylin into a temper. It was quite amazing to watch, and it made her more beautiful to him. But he also knew this was as far as he would go. She looked genuinely upset, her face all screwed up with indignation and concern. He wouldn't have it because of something he said.

"My mother used to say 'in a tiff' all the time," he said with a touch of sadness. "I guess it stuck with me. I'm sorry for insulting you, that wasn't my intention. And please call me Simon. May I still call you Aylin?"

"Ok. Fine. Yes. Wait a minute...you said your resort. As in, you are the manager and run the resort?" she asked.

"As in, this is my family's resort. While we all own a piece, I'm the one who owns a majority share and manages it on a day-to-day basis," Simon said as a matter of fact.

"Oh," she said, her eyes wide as she bit the corner of her lip.

"And as such, I would really like to know what happened so I can make things right for you," he said softly. No need to continue teasing her. He really wanted to know what was going on at his resort that would bring her in yelling it down.

"Someone threw a potted plant at my cabin door. It dented the door and broke all over the front step."

"Show me." Simon said as he rose from his chair and held out a hand toward Aylin.

She stared at his hand for a moment before putting her own into it, letting him pull her out of the chair and out the door. If her hand felt a little more comfortable in his than he would have liked, then he would need to deal with it later. He already admitted to himself he was attracted to her. Right now, though, wasn't the right time. Someone vandalized his cabin, and he needed to know why.

5

He wasn't only the hot resort manager. He was the hot resort owner!

Aylin thought about what it would be like to have him hold her. Just holding his hand for a minute in his office sent her tingling all over. How would it feel if she leaned in toward him and wrapped her arms around his waist? Would he wrap his arms around her, too, or push her away?

She watched Simon as they walked out of his office. The small lines around his eyes made him seem like someone who enjoyed life a lot, laughing as he did in his office. The laugh never really reached his eyes though. That, along with how serious he was now, made her wonder what took away his joy. Maybe it was the weight of owning and running a resort. She'd never had that much responsibility in her life, so she could only imagine how much pressure it was to have it.

She was reminded of when she watched him in profile at the beach. He looked so serious then, too. Why did he seem sad even when he smiled and laughed? Aylin didn't know what Simon was dealing with, but his whole tone was wistful when he mentioned his mother earlier.

When they exited his office, Simon turned down the hall in

the opposite direction from the lobby where they had originally come from earlier. "Isn't the way back to the lobby that way?" Aylin said, pointing toward her right down the hall.

"Yes, but we're going out the back. I have a golf cart we can take to your cabin."

Aylin thought that was more convenient, but wasn't the point of living out here about enjoying the walk through the woods? Of course, this was probably not the time for it. They needed to figure out why someone was throwing things at her cabin.

This wasn't a date. They weren't about to take a romantic stroll through the woods to her cabin. If only she could remind her heart. It kept on stuttering every time she looked at him.

Simon directed her out of the building to a covered area off the back of the resort, with several golf carts sitting in a row. He walked over to the wall next to the carts, opened a box with a code, pulling out a key before climbing onto the one unplugged cart sitting away from the others that were all plugged in.

Following his lead, she slid into the seat next to him. He started the golf cart up, pulled out of the parking spot, and headed down a path next to the resort that led to the cabins.

"Don't you need to know which cabin is mine?" she asked.

"No."

"Do you always know where everyone is staying?" she asked.

"I do. The main resort has ten rooms in total on the two upper floors, so I make a point to always know who is staying in which one. As for the cabins, we only have three right now, though I'm planning on adding two more in the off season."

"So I'm staying in..." Aylin trailed off, looking at him expectantly.

Simon laughed, "Hmmm...a test. You are in cabin B, located a little more toward the water, though not too close. In cabin A, you have Mr. Foster, who, like you, seems to want to spend most of his time secluded in his cabin. In cabin C, Ms. Irwin checked in yesterday," he rattled off.

"Well, it appears that you do know. More than me, actually. I saw the man, but haven't been out of my cabin to know who checked into the other one."

Aylin detected the pointed look Simon gave her before turning back to the path. Yes, she spent way too much time secluding herself into one place to write. Once she came out of it, she could let it all go and enjoy her life. Besides, she had fun whenever she was writing. It was what she did for a living, after all. And Aylin was not one to do things she didn't enjoy.

"You know, you really should name the cabins something more interesting than Cabin A, B, and C," she said wryly.

At the end of the path, Simon stopped the golf cart near her cabin. "Some of my cousins said the same thing. Feel free to throw out suggestions."

They got out of the golf cart and Aylin followed him over to her cabin door. It almost seemed worse to her now that she was seeing it again, now from a different angle.

"So this is what I was talking about. I'm not even sure where the potted plant came from because the ones around this cabin are yellow," she said, letting her voice taper off. Aylin didn't notice that before.

Were all the pots used to decorate the cabins the same color? They couldn't be, if this one thrown at her door was blue. It was the same design as the ones around her cabin, except for the color. Unless someone picked it up from another location all together. But that meant it was an even more deliberate act.

Crouching down over the mess with Simon, Aylin wondered where the person was standing when the pot was thrown. The dent in the door was significant and much of the dirt and pottery shards were in one area, with only some of them scattered further out. The person who threw this was very close to the door. If it was thrown from further away, the debris would have been more scattered.

"Well, it is a mystery, but that's what you like best, isn't it?" Simon asked, turning to her.

"I write crime fiction," she murmured, still looking around.

"This will certainly fit."

She turned her head back to Simon, throwing out her hand to point toward the doorstep. "How could you think this is some sort of crime? It's probably just kids fooling around."

"We don't get things happening like this here from kids. Mostly kids around here are too busy on the lake during the summer."

"Well, I'm still not—" A higher pitched 'Hello there!' coming from behind them cut her off mid-sentence.

They quickly stood and turned around to face a man and woman who were walking over from cabin A.

Cabin A had blue pots. Aylin could just make them out from behind the pair and some woods that separated the two cabins.

Why didn't she catch that before?

"Hi, I'm Deanna. I'm staying in cabin C. And this here is Chris. He's over there in cabin A. I was coming around to say hi to my summer neighbors," she said in greeting. "Wow! That is quite a mess. Have an accident?"

Deanna's sugary sweetness was already grating on Aylin's nerves. Something about her seemed too deliberate, but that was probably because she spent too much time on her own and not enough time getting out meeting people. Or so her friend, Angeline, told her all the time.

"Hi, I'm Aylin. This is Mr. Kerrigan. He manages the resort," Aylin said, giving Simon her own pointed look. She didn't know what it was, but she didn't feel comfortable with Deanna. And Chris was just glowering at them like he wanted to be left alone even though he came over to them.

"Hello, Ms. Irwin and Mr. Foster. I hope you are enjoying your stay." The man reluctantly shook Simon's hand when he held it out.

The woman had no such problem and reached out both of her hands to surround Simon's, holding on for a bit too long. "Oh, I'm having a wonderful stay, Mr. Kerrigan. But, please, call me Deanna."

He removed his hands, adding, "I'm glad to hear it. Please let my staff know if either of you needs anything during your stay."

She didn't understand why Deanna Irwin got to her or why she felt off when the woman touched Simon. She understood one thing, though. Chris Foster made her extremely uncomfortable, and she had to get out of there. "It was great to meet you, but we really need to get going. There are still some things we need to discuss up in Mr. Kerrigan's office."

"Oh sure. There will be plenty of time to hang out and talk later."

"Um...sure," she hesitantly agreed.

Aylin put her hand around the crook of Simon's arm, slightly nudging him toward the golf cart.

"Good afternoon. Enjoy your stay," he remarked.

"Thank you..." Deanna said, leaving it hanging, as if hoping he would give her his first name. But she moved Simon toward the golf cart quickly to prevent any more conversation. They got onto the golf cart and waved as Simon turned it back toward the resort.

6

Simon wondered what that was all about, but he wasn't about to question it in front of the others. Aylin had a fascinating mind. He didn't tell her, but he read all of her books and found them about as intriguing as he found her. They left him wondering about the person who wrote them. To put that much detail into a book. It made him feel as though he was living it with the characters. It had to mean the person writing it experienced something similar, right?

Meeting her, he now wondered even more about her. Because she was not what he thought she would be. Intriguing, yes. Desirable, absolutely. He thought she surely would be more hardened. Instead, she had a measure of street smarts mixed with a softness that made him want to hold her to him—preferably in bed.

Once they were out of sight from the others, Simon asked what he was thinking. "What was that all about?"

"There's something about Deanna Irwin that's not right. I can't put my finger on it, but no one is that syrupy sweet while looking for a reaction. And she was waiting for a specific reaction from us. As for Chris Foster, he just makes me shudder."

"How so?" he asked.

"He stares at you and doesn't look like he wants to be there. Or for anyone to be there. I really can't explain it. I couldn't wait to get away from him."

Simon noticed how uneasy Aylin seemed while talking about Chris. He hadn't met him before today, though he made it a point to know a little about everyone who was staying at his resort. He could not meet all the guests right away. Simon also heard nothing bad about Chris Foster from any of his staff. But he would ask them about their impressions later.

"Ok...we'll table the talk about him for now. But a lot of women act like Deanna. They put on a show to get what they want. Nothing new there."

"And I'm sure you get a lot of that, huh?" she asked, with a bit of snark thrown in.

"Care to explain that comment?" Simon asked, confused by what she meant by her question.

"Just that you're a good-looking guy who owns and runs a resort. You must have women putting on a show for you all the time to get your attention."

"Interesting. You've known me for an entire hour and decided I'm a good-looking guy and a shallow one at that." Simon couldn't help but rile Aylin up again. For some reason, it revved him up. Not that he should be revved up by one of his guests. He couldn't help himself.

"Oh no! That's not what I meant! I don't think you are shallow. Not that I really know you enough to say that for sure."

Simon laughed, "It's ok...I was just riling you up."

"Why would you do that?" she asked, her face all scrunched up in confusion.

"Because you're cute when I do," he said with a small smile.

"Cute! Cute! Ugh...puppy dog words."

Simon laughed again. He couldn't remember the last time he laughed so much. Especially in the last few months. Arriving back at the main building, Simon parked the golf cart, and they walked to his office together, closing the door.

"So you missed one big thing, Simon," she said as she sat down.

"And what was that?" He moved around his desk to sit behind it.

"The pot thrown at my door was blue."

"And..." he said, drawing out the word. He didn't know where she was going with that. Who cared what color the pot was?

Aylin shook her head in what he could only identify as exasperation, because he wasn't getting her point. Seriously, what difference did it make that the pot was blue? It was still lying in pieces on her cabin doorstep and had created more work for his staff, along with the damage to the door itself.

"You're not very observant for someone who knows everyone who is staying at your resort."

Simon stared at Aylin. Insulting him would not get them anywhere. After getting the hint that he would not fall for it, Aylin continued. "The pots at my cabin are yellow. The pots at cabin C are green. And the pots at cabin A are blue. The potted plant came from Chris Foster's cabin."

Well damn! Aylin was right. He really wasn't being very observant.

"That still doesn't mean that Chris Foster was the one to throw it at your cabin," he pointed out.

"True, but now that we know where it came from, we can figure out who."

Simon thought that was a horrible idea. No way was he going to let a guest get involved in investigating a potential crime. Especially not her. "No. I'll call someone to go over to your cabin to clean up the mess. While that's being done, you can grab some lunch or take a walk or something before you go back to your cabin to write. There will be no investigating."

Before she could respond, Simon's phone rang. He glanced at it both in annoyance and in relief. The last thing he wanted to do was deal with work right now, but he was also glad to cut off this conversation of figuring out who threw the pot at Aylin Miller's cabin door.

Sure he was curious. Someone upset his guest—even if he was feeling like she could be more than a guest to him—and damaged his property. He would call his cousin, Luke, who was the local sheriff, and file a report to be on the safe side. Other than that, he really couldn't waste his time investigating what happened.

The phone rang again before Simon answered it. Seeing it was a call coming from the kitchen, he answered with a gruff "hello" instead of his regular greeting of "Cypress Bay Manor Resort."

"Simon, you need to do something about Dad. I'm getting complaints from my waitstaff that he's trying to take over the dining room decor, and I'm up to my elbows in meal prep for the resort guests."

Simon closed his eyes for a moment as he listened to his brother. Oliver ran the resort's kitchen and was a fabulous chef —not that he'd tell him so. No need to swell his head any more than it already was.

"I'm a little busy right now, but I'll take care of it as soon as I'm done here."

"We need to do something to keep Dad busy and out of our hair. Let's get together tonight and come up with a plan."

"Good idea. 9 o'clock, my apartment?"

"I'll be there," Oliver said before hanging up.

"I can see that you're busy, so I'll just be going then. That lunch sounds like a good idea. I can't remember the last time I ate. I get so wrapped up in my work that I sometimes forget," she said, jumping out of the chair.

Simon glanced up at Aylin. She was looking at him as though she couldn't get out of his office quick enough. She turned and hurried to the door, her hand grabbing the doorknob.

"Hold up." He got up and walked over to her, putting his hand over hers on the doorknob, preventing her from turning it. "First, promise me you won't be investigating who threw that pot at your door on your own."

"Why would I do that? It was directed at me. Why wouldn't I want to at least keep my eye on the guy who may have thrown it?"

"Because whoever threw the pot could then hurt you. Plus, I'll be calling the sheriff to report the incident. Just to be on the safe side." The thin line of her lips told Simon that she wasn't happy with him telling her what to do. He waited for her to answer him.

"Fine," she grudgingly said.

At that, Simon gave her hand a quick squeeze before removing his hand from hers. She opened the door and was about to walk out when a thought occurred to him. He couldn't just let her go. He had to see her again.

"Have lunch with me tomorrow," he threw out, surprising himself with the request.

"What?" she asked, turning back to face him in surprise.

"Come over to the dining room tomorrow and have lunch with me. We can discuss who we think threw the pot and figure it out together." Simon knew it was a lie. He didn't want to discuss this any more, but he also understood it would grab Aylin's attention.

"Sure, why not," she agreed, then turned and walked out the door, this time turning toward the lobby. Simon didn't know what came over him, but somehow he needed to keep her close.

He sent a quick text to Luke reporting the incident along with some pictures he took while at the cabin, asking how long it would take from Luke's end. Getting the confirmation he would stop by in a few minutes to check it out, Simon stopped by the front desk to arrange for clean-up at the cabin.

Now all he had to do was find his father to take care of that mess before it got out of hand...again.

7

Well, whoever the person was that Simon was meeting tonight in his apartment, it didn't seem to be serious, considering he asked her out to lunch tomorrow. Not that she was jealous. She wasn't. And she definitely did not want a relationship of any kind with Simon. With anyone. She just wanted to write her book, have the Philadelphia police tell her it was safe, then go home.

Besides, Simon was not the right person for her. He was too tied to the resort. There was no way she would upend her whole life for another person. Aylin laughed at herself. Now she imagined a life with a man she literally just met a few hours ago.

Nice, Aylin! What next? A home with a white picket fence, a bunch of kids and a dog?

Right. That was so not her. She liked her life as it was. On her own. In her apartment that she was not currently living in, where she could write any time she wanted without having to worry about another person around.

Yes, that was exactly what she wanted and how she liked it. And if she would just keep telling herself that, then maybe she would believe it one day. She didn't need an incredibly handsome man who made her heart beat fast and her whole body vibrate whenever he was around. She didn't!

At that thought, her stomach growled, sounding like an angry cat—a giant one, who likely prowled and chased antelope. Aylin took Simon's suggestion and grab something to eat. It was getting late after all, and this wasn't the first time her stomach had been giving her hints. She really must schedule breaks into her day to eat.

Instead of thinking about everything going on around her, she would grab a late lunch—or maybe it was now an early dinner—and then go back to her cabin to write some more until she got tired. Aylin went toward the dining room of the resort, intent on getting a meal and finally quieting her stomach.

Noticing the sign at the entrance to Tola Dining that said to sit anywhere, she chose a small table next to the window where the lake was visible in the distance.

"Welcome to Tola Dining. I'm Billie and will be your server today. What can I get you to drink?" The server, wearing black pants and a white polo shirt with the Cypress Bay Manor Resort logo, asked while handing her a laminated menu.

"Hi, Billie. First, here's my dining card." Angeline had set up her stay where all her meals were comped to her cabin. When she checked in, they gave her a dining card to use at any of the resort's dining facilities. The waitstaff only had to swipe it when putting her order into their handheld devices, assigning it to her cabin. Aylin had her credit card charged automatically on a weekly basis to pay for them. It was a convenient arrangement available for those who stayed long term, and she was glad they offered it.

Quickly looking at the menu, she found it had a wide range of options, from sandwiches and salads to full dinner meals and pastas. And those options weren't what most would consider typical. Oh, sure, many of them were what you could find in just about any restaurant chain. But they also had options that looked like they came from a high end place where everyone wore suits and gowns to dinner.

She found her favorite listed and told Billie she was ready to order. "I'll have the BLT with fries and water with lemon. No need to bring the water first, Billie. I can wait until my meal is ready."

Billie swiped her dining card and handed it back before tapping away at the device in her hands. "Good choice, Ms. Miller. I'll be right back with your order," she said, walking away.

Aylin looked around the resort's dining room, which was slightly curved and painted in a brownish red color had a wall of windows encased in white decorative moulding, a nod to its Victorian-like roots she supposed. It would have felt closed in with the darker color, if it wasn't for the size of the room and how the light flowing through the windows gave it an open and comfortable vibe. The floor appeared to be wood, but on closer inspection, she realized it was tile that resembled wood. It must be a lot easier to clean.

Tables of varying sizes in dark wood were scattered around the room, some small with two chairs like the one she was sitting at now, others mid-sized with four chairs and a couple of larger tables in the center with six chairs. A long mahogany buffet table spanned one entire wall. She imagined they would use that for parties, though she really didn't know for sure.

In the back of the room, two sets of double swinging doors —most likely leading in and out of the kitchen area—along with a drink station, tucked into the space between each set of doors. Billie was working on filling up a tray with a bunch of drinks. Since there were only two couples in the dining room with Aylin right now, she assumed the server was getting all the drinks at once.

Turning back toward the windows, the view of the lake was nice to look at. The sun glowed over the water, boats came and went, Simon argued with another man. Whoa...wait a minute. That was Simon with an older man, and it did seem like they were arguing.

"Here you go, Ms. Miller." Billie said, setting her drink and meal in front of her, breaking her concentration of what was going on outside.

"Thank you, Billie. Do you know who that man is with Simon Kerrigan?"

"Oh, that's his father. Poor guy lost his wife recently, and he's been having some problems dealing with it. He was supposed to be retired, but he keeps coming in trying to work."

"I'm sorry to hear about his wife," Aylin murmured, continuing to watch the two outside.

"She was a wonderful woman. We were all upset when she died, but Simon held us all together, making sure the place stayed open and everyone had someone to talk to if they needed it." Billie noticed someone else coming into the dining room and excused herself, telling Aylin to enjoy her meal.

It seemed like Simon was taking care of many people. He always knew who was staying where. He came to help her right away. The phone call in his office gave her a different meaning now.

"I wonder who takes care of him," Aylin muttered to herself, watching first the man and then Simon walk away out of her sight.

After finishing her meal, she walked back to her cabin, where she found the pot cleaned up from her cabin stoop. A small dent was still on her door, but all the dirt and broken pieces of pottery, as well as the plant, were gone.

Running her finger lightly over the dent in the door, Aylin opened it and went inside, closing and locking the door behind her. It was time to continue her work. She lost too much time dealing with what she thought of as the pottery incident.

Walking back into the bedroom, where her desk and computer were set up, Aylin examined the wall with her notes and scene cards. Quickly reading through them, inspiration hit and Aylin got back to work.

8

After stopping by the front desk to have them call for someone to clean up the mess on Aylin's doorstep, Simon went in search of his father. The last thing he needed was to become responsible for his father and his actions at the resort. The man was supposed to be retired. But he knew his father was hurting after losing Simon's mother. Simon and his brother, Oliver, were hurting, too.

But they had something to keep them busy all day. What did their father have? He was supposed to spend his retirement with his wife, traveling and enjoying his life now that all the hard work was done.

Simon needed to take it easy with his father. But he also knew this couldn't go on. His father was messing with the resort and their employees' ability to do their own jobs. Not finding him in the kitchen, he went back into the lobby. Simon asked an employee passing by if they'd seen his father. She told him she thought he went outside and to check with maintenance.

He didn't like the sound of that. Maintenance was Ryleigh's domain, and he didn't need those two getting into it.

"Uncle John, I know you want to help, but I've got this."

"You know, Ryleigh, if I just hold this right here, you can get into..."

"Uncle John! Oh crap. Now look what happened!"

Simon ran around the corner of the building in time to see water spraying all over Ryleigh from a pipe in the ground.

"Whoa! Having a minor problem here?" Simon asked, giving Ryleigh a stern expression.

Ryleigh returned it right back, water dripping from her clothes and hat, before glancing back at his father with a sigh. "No. No problem here. Maybe you and Uncle John can go deal with that other thing."

"Other thing? What's going on, Simon? Is there a problem?"

Though frustrated and angry, Ryleigh was also aware of how much his father was hurting. It still didn't help that she would need to work more to fix something that should have been a quick fix.

"No problem, Dad. But let's go over by the lake and let Ryleigh fix the sprinkler line." Simon looked over at his cousin, mouthed the word 'sorry', then walked over to his father, where they continued to walk toward the lake.

His father really was becoming a menace. Simon was aware his father loved the resort. He spent his entire life here. But he was not in the right frame of mind to be getting involved with the daily work their employees were doing around the resort.

The resort had several family members who came in and out doing various jobs for them. They all had a stake in the running of it, but not all of them worked at the resort or did work full-time for them. As of right now, the only family working full time besides himself were his brother, Oliver, who ran the kitchen and dining areas; and their cousin, Marinda, who was not only Ryleigh's triplet with their other sister, Katia but also ran their customer relations and front desk.

Ryleigh was a handy woman extraordinaire. She could

build or fix anything. She regularly came in whenever the resort had a problem and often put in about ten hours or so of work each week. The rest of the time, she worked around town and put in time with her own small construction company.

The other cousins all had their own jobs away from the resort. Noah was a doctor at the hospital, though he split time with the local clinic. He went away for medical school and graduated early before coming back to take his place next to the town's only doctor.

Noah's twin brother, Luke, was the sheriff. He was in the Army—some sort of secret shit he couldn't pry a word out of him about. Injured, Luke eventually left the military to run for sheriff.

Hailee owned a book and tea shop in town. She was an only child, adopted as a baby by his Uncle Joshua and Aunt Felicia, who couldn't have a child of their own.

And finally, Katia, the middle triplet of Marinda and Ryleigh. She ran a deli and sandwich shop in town.

They would all drop what they were doing, emergencies aside for Noah and Luke, and come help at the resort. That's just how their family worked. As for ownership of the resort, they collectively made decisions on all major issues at their quarterly resort meetings. But daily day-to-day decisions were made by him alone, though he did frequently ask for opinions, especially by his department managers.

When they got halfway to the lake, his father stopped and turned toward him. "Okay. I know what you're going to say, but this is my resort as much as, if not more than, yours. I can help wherever I want."

"Dad, you retired and turned the resort over to us to run. And while we still respect the work you and Mum put into the resort, you cannot do whatever you want to do here anymore."

"Well, I un-retire then. I think it's time I come back full time and ran the place with you."

"You can't do that. All the legal paperwork was filed years ago and you are now only a figurehead of the resort. If you want to work, we can find a position for you, but you need to stop bothering our staff trying to do their jobs."

"I don't want you to find a position for me. I am this resort! Those employees you say I am bothering don't know what they are doing and I am going to continue to make sure they are doing their jobs here correctly!" John yelled before stomping away.

Simon watched his father walk away with a heavy heart. They had to do something about him. Oliver needed to help him come up with some solutions tonight because he didn't know if he could find a way to help his father on his own.

Walking away in the other direction, he reminded himself he couldn't control his father or his actions. Wanting to think about something else, his mind drifted to thoughts of Aylin.

She was getting inside his head too much already. He wasn't sure he liked it. Simon admitted, though, it was pleasant having someone around who made him laugh again. She was intriguing to him, that's all. She wasn't half bad to look at either. Fine, she was a knockout. All those soft curves, her auburn hair, and those eyes—they really got him thinking about what it would be like having her under him. What color would they be when she was aroused?

Realizing where his thoughts were going, he shook his head. He couldn't be thinking about a guest that way. Other than as a guest with a problem to solve, he should forget all about her and that fabulous body, her quick and witty mind.

Bloody hell! Thinking about her as a guest only would not be easy at all.

9

She was floating above the beach by the lake, standing upright, her feet inches from the sand. Looking down, she realized she was wearing a long, flowing nightgown and no shoes. That was strange. She never wore anything like this. Ever. Her normal attire was some sleep shorts and a large t-shirt.

Shrugging, she looked around. The resort's dock and gazebo were in the distance, a lone man standing as though waiting for her. Could she walk to him? She couldn't even feel the sand on the bottom of her feet. Giving it a try, she quickly realized she could walk, as though her feet were touching the ground. It was like walking on a pocket of air. Her pace was quicker than in real life, too. Apparently, distance in dream life meant she only had to take a couple of steps before she was where she wanted to go.

She stepped up behind the man, willing him to turn. As he did, she could make out his profile features. Simon. She opened her arms to him as he turned and—"

A loud bang shook the cabin and jolted her awake, abruptly ripping Aylin from her dream.

"What? What happened? What was that?" Aylin blearily glanced at the clock on the table next to the bed and groaned.

Three a.m. It was way too early for loud bangs. Besides the dream, she had barely slept thinking about Simon, the argument she saw him having with his father, and wanting to drag him off to her bed. It would never happen.

Disoriented, she dragged herself out of bed, grabbing the robe hanging on the bedpost along the way.

"This better be some animal knocking around the cabin," she said out loud to herself, putting on her robe and belting it around her waist.

Not wanting to open the door this late at night—because that was what all the crazy psycho killers wanted a woman living on her own to do—Aylin peaked out the back windows first. There wasn't anything but darkness and some of the moon shining through the trees.

Walking to the front of the cabin, she moved the edge of the curtain away from the front window next to the door. It was just as dark as the back, but it seemed different. The moonlight was visible, but only in parts of the window. The rest appeared dark, almost like there was a film over the window.

Going over to the other window, further away from the door in the kitchen area, Aylin repeated the process of moving the edge of the curtain away to peek out. Through this window, she could clearly see the moonlight without any kind of film.

Okay, so it seemed like whatever that bang was, left something covering one of her windows. Looking out the window toward the other window and doorstep, there was something resembling a dark blob covering the area.

Not knowing what it could be, her imagination began to run wild. Was there an animal attack on another animal, leaving a bloody mess all over her cabin? Or maybe it attacked a person! She wasn't thrilled with her cabin neighbors, but she wouldn't want anything like that to happen to them!

"Calm down, Aylin. No need to think the worst. So what should I do? Look outside my door to make sure there isn't anyone out there needing medical help? Or call the resort and let them know there may be someone outside needing medical help?" she asked herself out loud.

Aylin took a few deep breaths to calm herself down. She would just take a quick peek outside first. No need to wake the entire resort with an imaginary emergency. Or make them thinking the fiction crime writer staying in the cabin by herself was losing her mind, or bringing her books to life for some sort of attention or something. Imagine if she called, and they found nothing outside.

Decision made, Aylin grabbed the flashlight from the kitchen drawer she found the other day. It would not only give her some light to see what was going on, but was heavy enough to act as a weapon if a wild animal was out there waiting for her. Not that she would get close enough to hit it. Throwing it at the animal to scare it away wasn't out of the option.

She quietly unlocked the door, slowly opening it a crack, then pointing the flashlight outside and moving it around looking for anything or anyone out there. Not seeing anyone, she opened the door further and pointed the flashlight toward the ground, where she caught sight of a bunch of blue paint.

"What the hell!"

She peered around the door frame, turned the flashlight around to face the window, showing more blue paint, and even more on the front door, when she turned to look at it. It was everywhere—splattered on every surface—thick, oozing, and sticky blue paint dripped down the door, windows, and stairs.

Not wanting to get the paint on herself or have it drip inside the cabin, she closed the door and turned off the flashlight, putting it down on the small table under the windows.

Was this connected to the broken pot the other day? Was it connected to what happened to her at home? Did the stalker find her? No, that couldn't be. No one knew she was in Florida except for her parents and Angeline. Besides, she wanted to leave that behind her while she was here.

The Philadelphia police were taking care of the stalking issue, with Angeline checking in with them every once in a while and giving her updates. Evidently, all had been quiet back home since she left. No more letters, no more phone calls to her or her publisher, no more break-ins. It was as though the stalker had left when she did.

No! She would not think that way. The stalker probably got scared off by her neighbor while breaking into her apartment. No need to bring all that mess up to Simon or anyone else. It was not related to the stalker.

"I need to call the resort and let them take care of this mess. It's probably more kids...that's all." Aylin tried to convince herself, but deep down, she had her doubts.

10

The phone ringing two hours after he got to bed was the first sign his day would not go as planned. Simon had spent most of the evening with Oliver, figuring out what to do with their father. They hashed out potential areas where he could work at the resort to keep him busy and what to do if he decided he didn't want to do that task.

They also argued about who should shoulder the responsibility of their father. Oliver saying that Simon ran the resort, so he should take care of anything dealing with it and Oliver would take care of anything their father needed when he was at home. Simon thought they would share all the responsibility of their father. They spent most of their time at the resort, after all.

Oliver shut down as usual, and Simon may have said some things he now regretted. Like how he and their cousins always called Oliver 'stone-cold' because he never seemed to show what he was feeling or want to get involved in anything too emotional. But Simon knew Oliver tended to feel too much, and so he locked down his emotions to keep from getting too overwhelmed. At least until he couldn't hold it in anymore, then everyone should stand back.

"Hello," he answered the phone groggily.

"Simon, I'm sorry to disturb you this late at night, but we received a call about an incident over at Cabin B," the night clerk, Tiffany said.

Simon sat up quickly, looking around for some clothes to throw on. "I'll be right there. And have Allen grab me one of those portable spotlights from the storeroom." He hung up and got a pair of light gray sweatpants and a sleeveless t-shirt from his closet that he often used for working out at the resort's gym. Throwing them on, along with some socks and sneakers, Simon grabbed his keys and phone before walking out his apartment door.

Ten minutes later, he was standing in front of Aylin's cabin looking at the blue paint splattered all over the door, steps, side of the cabin, and window. A gallon paint can sat in the flower bed, tipped at an angle and dug into the dirt, obviously thrown with force.

Aylin strode around the cabin and stopped next to him, looking at the paint splatter that was illuminated by the portable spotlight he set up nearby.

"Looks like one of those inkblot psychological tests," she mused.

Simon eyed Aylin curiously and wondered what she was talking about and why she was so calm.

"You know the ones where they show you an inkblot and you have to tell them what you see in it, like a butterfly or a moth, or something," she said, trailing off as he continued to stare at her. "It's blue again."

"I noticed that," Simon said as he examined the cabin again. "Tell me what happened."

"I was asleep and heard another loud bang." She wasn't

about to tell him about the dream she was having. "But this one shook the entire cabin, which woke me up, obviously."

"Obviously."

"I wasn't about to become a statistic, so I looked out the windows before peeking out the door, saw the paint, and decided to call it in. I didn't have your direct number, so I called the front desk."

"Why would you become a statistic?" She baffled him sometimes. Simon wasn't sure what was going on inside Aylin's mind half the time he spoke with her.

"Oh, you know, in books or movies there is always that too stupid to live person who rushes to open the door to the killer waiting for her on the other side."

"Your mind obviously takes you straight into one of your books."

"Obviously," she replied dryly, making Simon smirk.

Despite their easy banter, the incidents occurring to Aylin and her cabin puzzled and concerned Simon. At first, he chalked it up to an accident — someone playing around trying to scare the cabin occupant. Now it felt a little too directed toward Aylin. He needed to know more about what was going on, and he needed to know now.

"This seems like it's more than kids at this point. Has anything like this happened to you before?"

Not looking at him, Aylin mumbled something below her breath, then said, "No, nothing like this has happened before."

Simon stared at Aylin a little more. There was something she wasn't telling him. She wouldn't look at him anymore, seeming to be more interested in looking around the cabin than at him.

"Aylin," he said sternly, still staring at her. Her head popped up, and she looked hesitantly at him. "What aren't you telling me?"

"Nothing. Now, can we figure out who is doing these things

soon? I came here to finish my book and I can't work if I'm wondering if something else is going to happen," she replied testily.

"Sure. No problem." He didn't believe a word she said. Something was going on that she didn't want to tell him. He'd give her some time, but he would keep a close watch over her. If she brought trouble with her to his resort, then he would find out. "Let me call Luke and have him come over to document this. Then I'll have someone come clean up this mess."

"Great...you do that. I'm going back in," Aylin said as she walked away.

"I'll see you for lunch this afternoon," he called out. Her steps stuttered a bit before she raised her hand in acknowledgement and walked away around the cabin, where he assumed she'd enter from the back glass doors. He'd believe this didn't affect her, if he didn't witness the fear and vulnerability she briefly showed in her eyes before shuttering them.

Pulling out his phone, Simon called his cousin Luke to inform him of another incident. "Luke, sorry to wake you so early, but we have another problem at the cabins."

"No worries, I was already up. What kind of problem?"

"Someone threw blue paint all over the front of the cabin. Forcefully."

"I'm on it," Luke said, hanging up. Simon was used to Luke and how he was very succinct and to the point. Not wanting to keep attention on the cabin while he waited, he turned off the spotlight, leaving it in place and turned on his flashlight instead to wait for Luke.

Chris Foster walked out of the trees surrounding his cabin, startling Simon. He cursed himself for not being more aware of his surroundings.

"Hello, Mr. Foster. Taking a late night walk?" Simon inquired. He wanted to keep an eye on Chris. Once Aylin told him how she felt around the man, he noticed something off about him as well. Again, nothing specific he could put his finger on, but there was something slightly creepy about the man.

Chris leaned against a tree on the outskirts of the area between his cabin and Aylin's, crossing his arms. "I saw all the lights and was wondering what was going on."

"Someone vandalized your neighbor's cabin. You have any trouble over your way?" Simon mirrored the man's pose on the opposite side of the clearing.

"Nope, no problems at my cabin. Sounds like the writer is attracting some trouble," he sneered.

"Hmmm...possibly," he said, watching Chris suspiciously. Simon was looking for any kind of reaction that would show he was the one who had been vandalizing Aylin's cabin.

His face was a mask, showing nothing but a small sneer. Of course, Simon could be wrong. It wasn't like he was trained to recognize when someone was hiding something. He'd leave that to Luke.

"I called the sheriff, so he should be here soon. I'm sure he'll want to speak with you and Ms. Irwin to check if you've seen anything in the area lately."

"Sure. Anytime. I think I'll go back to bed. Good night," Chris said nonchalantly before unfolding his arms and moving his body off the tree.

Simon watched Chris Foster walk back toward his cabin further in the woods, wondering if he just talked with the person responsible.

Standing in the shadows of the woods, the culprit stared at Simon and the cabin. Anger radiated out, making the air shudder around anyone nearby.

That bitch thinks calling Mr. Kerrigan will save her. Ha! Nothing can save her!

And if he thinks the sheriff will solve the mystery—save that horrible woman from her fate? Never!

They could call anyone they wanted and they would still have no idea what was going on. They won't be able to figure it out or stop what needed to be done.

Aylin Miller's days were getting short. And she didn't even know it.

She would pay for what she did to me!

11

That afternoon, Simon knew he would need to pick up Aylin for lunch. He was already figuring her out. She got so involved in her work that she often forgot to eat or that there was anything else going on around her except her writing. Passing by the lobby front desk, he heard someone call out to him.

Turning, he saw his cousin at the front desk. "Hey Marinda. Working the desk this morning?"

"Meredith's kid was sick this morning, and she had to take her to the clinic. I'm only filling in until Corey can come in."

"That's too bad. Let me know how her daughter is when you find out."

"Sure. So what's this I've been hearing about some trouble recently? I haven't heard the specifics. Anything I need to know about?" While Marinda didn't take care of the minutiae of running the resort, she was still part owner. They had quarterly meetings together to talk about the resort, how it was doing, all the numbers, and to discuss any future plans.

Simon let out a small sigh. "Someone keeps on vandalizing cabin B."

"What!" Marinda stared at him in shock.

"First, it was a potted plant thrown at her door a couple of days ago. Early this morning, it was a can of blue paint thrown at the front of the cabin." Simon let out a deep breath. "We'll need to repaint the front of the cabin to repair it and perhaps paint the concrete steps, too."

"Do you think someone is targeting her? Those things seem so specific."

"It may be. I'm not sure we have the entire story yet. But I'm about to go pick her up for lunch, so we can figure out who may be involved. Though Luke is on it, too."

"Well, if Luke can't figure it out, then no one can."

"So right. I'll see you later, Marinda."

"Bye, Simon. Oh, and you'll be happy to know that I haven't seen Uncle John all day."

That was one piece of good news. "Great...thanks."

Simon walked out of the resort into a soupy summer heat. Perhaps he should have stayed in his workout clothes from this morning. Releasing the button around his right wrist, he rolled up his sleeve before doing the same to his left. He walked down the path to the cabins, feeling a little better now that his sleeves were rolled up, but not by much. They were just getting into the real heat and humidity of summer, even though it wasn't even June yet. By the time they got to August, Simon knew he would really complain about wearing dress pants and a button-down shirt.

Approaching the cabin, he examined the work that was already done to fix the destruction. Yellow tape cordoned off the area around the front of the cabin after the cleaners he hired mopped up almost all the blue paint, leaving a blue stain on the siding, door, and steps. The windows were clean, so there was that. And he took note that Luke had someone take the paint bucket, probably wanting to see what, if anything, they could get off it.

The painters were waiting for him to let them know it was alright to paint and he would do that right after lunch.

Simon and Luke tried to convince Aylin to move into the main resort while the work was being done, but she wouldn't budge an inch from the cabin. Telling them that all her stuff was already set up and she couldn't work with others banging their doors or making noise in the hallways all day. Simon told her their resort wasn't like that, but she wasn't having it.

He tried to tell Aylin the front door would be unusable for a while and she just said she would use the back sliding glass doors instead. So he walked around the cabin to knock on the glass doors to pick her up.

He knocked once sharply to get her attention and, after not getting a response, knocked harder and longer until she peeked around the corner of the bedroom door. "Come open the door and let's go to lunch."

"No," she said, shaking her head back and forth while still hiding behind the door frame.

"Aylin, don't you want to leave the cabin, eat, and talk about who you think is doing all this?" Simon really didn't have any plans to talk about who she thought was vandalizing her cabin. But he wanted to know more about her and if there was anything she wasn't telling him that may cause someone to target her.

"Ok. You want me to open the door?"

"Why else am I standing out here telling you to open the door?" Simon just didn't understand women sometimes. Why all the games? Just be straight forward about what you did or didn't want.

He about swallowed his tongue when she stepped out from behind the door. Dressed in only a towel wrapped about her body, Aylin walked over to the glass door and unlocked it. When he didn't move to open it, she pulled the door open.

"Are you coming in?"

"Ummm...yeah," he stuttered and took a step toward her, walking through the door as he stared at her.

The towel barely covered her breasts, hanging on by one little tuck of the corner between them. The end of it came to the top of her thighs. She was curvy in all the right places...breasts, hips, thighs. He wanted more than anything to rip the towel away from her and see what she looked like completely naked. Of course, he would never do that to a woman without her consent. Didn't mean Simon wasn't tempted.

"This is why I didn't want to let you in. I just got out of the shower and hadn't dressed yet, but since you insisted." She turned back toward her room. "I'm going to finish getting dressed, then we can go to lunch."

Simon let out a breath when she closed the bedroom door. Damn, she was even more than he thought she was. Round in all the right places, just like he loved in a woman. He wanted to wrap her up in his arms. She would fit right against his chest. His head resting on the top of hers.

When she suddenly opened the door, and walked out wearing jeans and a sleeveless buttoned shirt, it startled him out of his thoughts. He realized he had never moved from the spot while she changed. Standing in place, he stared at the bedroom door, letting his imagination think about what it would be like for them if they were together.

"I'm ready when you are."

"That was quick."

"Yeah, well, I don't need a lot of time getting ready. If someone doesn't like me as I am, wearing jeans and no makeup with wet hair, then they can turn right around and walk away."

"I won't be walking away." They stared at each other until she broke eye contact.

"Ok. Let's get going then."

They walked over to the glass doors and opened one of

them, walking outside. As she closed the sliding doors, she stood there looking confused.

"Finally figure out why I wanted you to stay at Cypress Manor while they clean up the mess out front?" Simon asked smugly.

"I don't know what you're talking about. There's nothing to figure out."

"The glass sliding doors don't lock from the outside, Aylin. It's not safe to leave them unlocked when you're gone from the cabin," he pointed out.

"It will be fine. You have people you trust around to clean up the cabin, so it will be safe enough while we go eat. I won't be leaving again after our lunch, so it's not a problem. Come on, let's go."

She rushed around the cabin to the front. Simon couldn't believe how cavalier she was being about her safety. But she was right about one thing. He had people coming around to clean up the cabin today. He would let them know to keep an eye on the back as well.

12

Aylin followed Simon into the resort's dining room to a table in the corner next to the windows, the server walking up to the table immediately to take their order. "Hi Simon, Ms. Miller. Can I get you something to drink while you decide what you want to eat?" Billie asked.

"I'll take a water with some lemon, please," she said.

"I'll take the same, Billie," Simon said with a smile for the server.

"Great! I'll be right back with them." Aylin watched the woman walk away toward the drink station as she fiddled with the menu in front of her.

Aylin wasn't comfortable with Simon staring at her anymore. It took a lot for her to open the door at her cabin in only her towel. It wasn't as if she was someone who liked to flaunt her body. She was way too introverted for that. But there was something about Simon that made her want to be bold with him.

"So, Sim—" she began.

"Here you go. Are you ready to order?" Billie placed their

drinks in front of them on the table, looking at them expectantly, waiting for their order.

"Umm, yes, I'll take the BLT and fries," she told the server.

It was the only thing she could order quickly without actually looking at the menu to see what else they had available. Thank goodness it was a favorite of hers. She could eat it for almost every meal if she had to.

"Tell me about yourself, Aylin," Simon said once he finished giving his order and Billie left.

"Um, there's not really a lot to tell."

"Where are you from? Do you have family?"

"I'm from Philadelphia. My parents live there too. Has your family always owned the resort?" Aylin hated talking about herself. She was more interested in what others had to say than hearing herself talk about her own life. And if he started prying into her life, then she might let it slip about the trouble she was having with the stalker back home.

He stared at her a little too long for her liking before answering her question. "Well, that's quite a story about my family and this resort. Are you sure you're interested in hearing it? I'm sure you are far more interesting."

"Yes, I would much rather know more about this resort and your family. You said you all own it? How many of you are there?" she asked.

"There are eight of us all together."

"You have seven siblings!"

"No," he replied, to her surprise with a chuckle. "One brother and a bunch of cousins. Now shoosh and let me finish the story."

He shooshed her! "Shoosh! Are you an eighty-year-old grandmother or something?"

"Just another thing my mother used to say all the time. Now listen," he admonished her, though humor sparkled in his eyes.

"Let's start at the beginning so you can understand where the eight came from. A long time ago, my paternal grandparents, John and Marinda Kerrigan, came to Florida from New York, where they helped build the town of Cypress Bay. A group of residents wanted it to be a tourist destination—a place some of the Orlando tourists would want to come visit away from the city. And so they pooled their money to develop it as a tourist lakeside getaway. One place they built was this resort, though it was smaller back then."

"If a group of residents built it, doesn't that mean it belongs to all of them? How did it become your family's?"

"I'm getting to that. Over time, my grandparents not only helped grow the town, but they also grew their family. Before they moved here to Florida, they already had my father, John Jr., and my Uncle Luke—we call him Uncle Lou. And so they needed a place to raise their family. They moved into the resort with their two small boys and planned on having more." Simon paused, taking another bite of his food.

He mesmerized Aylin and until he ate; she forgot all about her food. Actually, she didn't even realize Billie had been back and dropped it off. It must have been while Simon was talking. Picking up her sandwich, she took a large bite out of it.

"So what happened next?" she asked, mumbling with the food filling her mouth.

"Well, they had a set of twins next, my uncles, Joshua and Paul. All six of them lived in a much smaller section of the resort than what I have now in my apartment, but the boys were still small and it worked for them," he said with a shrug. "Eventually, the properties the group all invested in together became solely owned by those who ran them. Apparently, they had some clauses—which I won't get into— that allowed complete ownership after a certain amount of time, assuming the business ran a profit and was managed by those claiming ownership."

"Is that legal?" It didn't sound right to Aylin, but she wasn't a lawyer and did not know what was or wasn't legal in business.

"Probably not, but those were the rules they laid out and enforced. My grandparents met all the clauses and were given the resort outright. As time moved forward, they made sure the resort was legally theirs and that they could pass it down to their family. They had another boy after it became officially theirs, my uncle Riley."

"Ok. So with five boys, I can see where the eight cousins came from. Who belongs to who?" she asked.

"I have a brother, Oliver. Our parents are John Jr. and Lauren. Next are my twin cousins, Luke Jr. and Noah. They're the sons of Uncle Lou and Aunt Amanda. Uncle Joshua and Aunt Felicia couldn't have kids and so they adopted my cousin, Hailee, when she was a baby. Uncle Paul died when he was 13 from cancer, so I never got to meet him." Simon paused to take another bite of his food, prompting her to take a bite as well.

"That must have been devastating to everyone."

"Yes, it was. Or so I've heard. And then Uncle Riley had to show everyone up and have triplet girls."

"Triplets!"

"Yeah, Marinda, Katia, and Ryleigh. So that's how we got to eight of us."

"Yes, but if all your surviving uncles are still around, why don't they still own it?"

"They were never interested in running the resort, so as soon as their children became adults, they each transferred their ownership rights to them. Some of us wanted to work at the resort and some would rather own it in name only. It works for us."

"There's no fighting over who gets what?"

"Nope."

"Huh." Aylin would need to mull that over for a while. She was used to hearing about families breaking apart when it came to inheritances and contesting who owned what, especially something as big as a successful resort.

"So, Aylin, what can you tell me about the trouble we've been having?"

Aylin was so caught off guard by his question, she almost choked on her water. "What do you mean? What can I tell you?" He couldn't know what was going on. Could he?

"Perhaps I should reframe the question. Any ideas about why it seems you have been specifically targeted by someone wanting to vandalize my cabin?"

She took a moment to compose herself before answering. "Not at all. Do you really think I'm being targeted? Maybe it's kids. Or someone's confused about who is staying at my cabin. Maybe they meant to target another guest and got the cabin wrong."

"Hmmm...possibly." Simon said, not sounding very convinced. "Ready to go?"

"Go? Where are we going?"

"I meant, are you done eating?"

"Oh, yeah." She looked down and realized she had finished eating everything on her plate. If only she remembered eating it.

"Let's go. Do you mind if we go to my office for a bit before I walk you back to your cabin?"

"You don't need to walk me back to my cabin."

"Sure I do. I picked you up, so I need to drop you off, too. It's only right on a date," he nonchalantly said, getting up from the table.

"This is not a date," she insisted. But he wasn't listening to her anymore. He had already turned and started walking. Not knowing what else to do, she followed him.

Once they got to his office, he opened his door and ushered her inside. Aylin wasn't sure what happened next, but suddenly she was pressed against the closed door and Simon was kissing the hell out of her. His hands were resting on her cheeks, fingers speared into her hair, wrapping around her head, and his thumbs were caressing her jawline and under her chin.

It was the most erotic kiss she'd ever had. She lost herself in him, his touch, his scent, the feel of his tongue against hers.

"Sorry, I couldn't help it any more. Sitting across from you during lunch, all I could think about was kissing you," he murmured in between kisses.

"Hmmm. I've been thinking about you, too," she said, remembering her earlier dream.

"That's good."

"Is it?" Aylin moved away from Simon by shifting to the side, dislodging his hands from her face. "I'm not sure this is the best time for me."

It was so hard to move away. She had to, though. She didn't want to get involved with anyone while trying to finish up her book and until the issues she was having with her stalker went away. Add in what had been happening at the cabin and it made for more than she wanted to deal with.

It was going to be hard to stay away from him, but Aylin had to keep her distance from him, if this was the way it was going to be. She couldn't think when he touched her like that. And it was only a kiss! Her skin and lips still tingled all over. He would be too hard to resist if he touched her again.

"Ayl—"

"No, I need to go." She opened the door and bolted down the hallway, leaving him standing at the door watching her go.

13

"Have you ever heard of knocking?" Simon asked as his brother barged into his office later that day.

His brother's disruption annoyed him. He was desperately trying to keep Aylin off his mind by finishing up some paperwork. And it wasn't working. Oliver's presence made it even worse.

Oliver stepped back outside the office and knocked on the door, raising his eyebrow at him. "Good enough for you?" his brother asked sarcastically.

"Yeah, what's up?" Simon asked, shaking his head at his brother's antics. They never followed any sort of strict protocol with each other. He and his brother would frequently barge into each other's rooms as kids and if it wasn't for doors that locked, they would continue to do the same with their homes. He wasn't in the mood for it.

"Have you been able to talk to Dad yet?" Oliver asked.

"I haven't been able to find him to talk to him. It's like he's keeping a low profile, but I know he's around somewhere. Though no one has seen him."

Simon was also frustrated about not being able to connect with his father today. He was concerned about him and wanted his happy father back—he wasn't acting like himself. John Kerrigan, Jr. was still grieving the loss of Simon and Oliver's mother, but he thought it would have gotten better in the last few months. Instead, it had gotten worse.

"That's good enough for me. If we can't find him, that means he's not causing any problems," his brother casually said.

"What's this 'we'? I can't find him. I don't see you looking for him or telling him he can't keep getting involved with the resort and bothering our employees. Don't be a bloody git, Oliver." Simon was livid.

He was the one doing all the work when it came to their father. He was the one corralling him in more than Oliver. When was Oliver going to step up to help? Instead, all he was doing was coming to him to complain about their father.

His brother turned toward the door. "Whatever. I don't have time for this."

Oliver was shutting down right in front of him. His face void of any emotion. Letting out a deep breath, he understood he had to fix this. They were always close and this issue with their father was putting a wedge between them.

Oliver was always the one who avoided any kind of conflict and internalized his emotions, keeping them locked up tight. But since the death of their mother, he'd been worse. He knew Oliver was having a hard time letting out his emotions in a healthy way. Cooking seemed to help, but that meant he was frequently in the resort kitchen and not always available to help with their father.

At this rate, he would probably have a brand new menu for every season at the resort. Not that they had many seasons in Florida. Mostly, it was a blistering hot summer tourist season with a shorter, cold winter season. Still, he would not put it past his brother to make it seem like they had them with a varying menu.

"Wait, Oliver." His brother stopped at the door and slowly turned around. "I'll find Dad and take care of it. It's just all this vandalism happening with the cabin on top of Dad sticking his nose in everything. Well…"

"I know you are dealing with most of this, Simon," he interrupted. "I'll try to do better at helping with Dad, but it's bloody hard for me to see him so devastated. And I know what you're thinking…that I'm keeping it all in, too. I know I am. I'm getting there, okay?"

Simon nodded at Oliver as he left the office, closing the door behind him.

And what should he do now? Eyeing the unfinished paperwork on his desk, he knew he wouldn't be able to finish it. He'd leave it for later. It would still be sitting on the desk after work. Or he would do it tomorrow.

His two biggest priorities were dealing with his father and the vandalism on Aylin's cabin. And maybe he should throw Aylin in as a priority, too. Did he want that? Thinking about the kiss, he would have to say yes. She was his top priority and screw the rest!

Realistically, though, he could not get too deeply involved with her emotionally. Physically was another thing all together, but never emotionally.

She didn't know they were having dinner together yet, but she would soon. He had to keep their relationship to nothing more than lunches, dinners, and, hopefully, sex. Waiting until their dinner tomorrow would be soon enough to see and think about her.

For all he knew, Aylin was the one who brought the trouble with her. He had to figure out what was going on with the vandalism first, while taking care of his father. Then he could think about what was happening with Aylin.

Plan in place, Simon pulled out his phone to text Luke. It would be good to know if he had found out anything about the latest incident at the cabin.

Simon: Learn anything new?

Luke: Yes.

Simon: And?

Luke: Some guy asked a kid to buy the paint.

Simon: So, any leads on this guy?

Simon stared at his phone, waiting for an answer from Luke. When nothing came through, he figured Luke got pulled into something else.

It wasn't as though his cousin wasn't a busy man. As the county sheriff, Luke had to handle more than only resort business or any calls in Cypress Bay. He took care of the entire county, which included another office in Tola Beach across from Lake Tola. That meant he often had to drive around the lake or across the bridge to respond to calls or check in with his deputies, not only in Cypress Bay but also Pine Grove to the north, Riverview to the south, and Tola Beach to the west.

Unless it was an emergency, Luke would respond when he was good and ready to respond.

It was time to carry on with his day. Needing to find his father, Simon walked out of his office and down the hall. His phone vibrated in his pocket when he was almost to the lobby, so he stopped to check on what Luke had texted.

Luke: We have a paper with the paint color given to the kid. We need to match the handwriting. Will be by later.

Simon: Need help?

Guess he would see Aylin later tonight, after all.

<h1 align="center">14</h1>

Later that night, Aylin had an urge to talk to Angeline about Simon. She didn't want to tell her about what was happening at her cabin. The last thing she wanted was for her friend to worry more than was necessary.

Angeline was the type of person to take care of everyone. If she told her what was going on, she'd hop on the first flight available to Orlando. Then she would rent a car and drive to Cypress Bay to make sure in person that Aylin was alright. The apartment break-in was bad enough. This would throw her over the edge with worry.

Pressing her friend's number in her contacts, Aylin waited for her to answer while it rang.

"Aylin!" Angeline answered with excitement.

"Hi, Ang. How are things going at home?" she asked, hoping this would keep the subject off her for a bit.

"Everything is wonderful here, but I want to hear how you're doing in Cypress Bay. How's the writing going? And most importantly, have you met any gorgeously tanned Florida men?" Well, that didn't work out the way she wanted.

"The writing is going okay. I'm getting a lot done, but not as much as I would like right now."

"Is it because of a man?"

"What is it with you wanting me to meet a man? You know nothing can come of it anyway, and I need to spend my time writing, not mingling."

"First, you spend way too much time in your writing cave you call an apartment. This is the first time in a long time you've had the opportunity to meet someone who isn't your nosey body neighbor or the leering douchebag from down the hall."

Yeah...that guy was always looking at her funny whenever she came out of her apartment. Which she rarely did. Unless Angeline dragged her out, or she finally came up for air and realized she needed to buy groceries.

"Second, who says nothing can come of it? Even a hot Florida fling is better than what you've been getting lately. Which, if you've been paying attention, though not very likely, has been a big fat zero on the sex register."

"Sex register? What! My sex life is like a check register now? Do I need to balance my books?"

"If you had anything to balance, but there's been nothing and don't deny it," Angeline dryly said.

She was right. Aylin hadn't been on a date in forever and the last one ended up being more like a 'hanging out with friends' deal. Though she was never one to date much, always with a book in hand, or trying to find the next story to write. Maybe a fling wouldn't be so bad.

Her thoughts veered to Simon for a minute before she responded. "You're right—and don't let that go to your head—but I really do need to concentrate on my book."

"Of course you do, but that doesn't mean you can't have a passionate fling on the side in between writing sessions." Angeline should have been the writer instead of an editor. "And you still haven't answered my question. Have you met any gorgeously tanned men?"

Her friend had a one track mind today. "Well," she said, drawing out the word.

"Oh. My. God. You met someone! Tell, tell, tell."

Aylin rolled her eyes at her friend's middle school enthusiasm, even knowing she couldn't see it over the phone. They needed to set up a video call. She missed seeing her friend. This was the first time since they met she couldn't pop over to visit her any time she wanted.

"I kind of ran into the man who runs the resort, and he kind of owns it, and we ate lunch together, then went to his office where he kissed me senseless, but I left because I can't get involved with him and I have writing to do because that's what's important right now," she quickly said, slurring her words together and hoping Angeline only caught part of it.

"Ooookay. Let me make sure I have this straight. The hot resort owner—"

"I never said hot." Simon was totally hot.

"—kissed you in his office after lunch and you ran away because you think work is more important. Does that sound right?"

"It is important. That's why I came down here. To finish my book."

"Yes, you need to finish your book, but you went to Cypress Bay to escape a crazy stalker who broke into your apartment. You could do those things from anywhere," she said. "For example, you could have stayed with me, with your parents, or rented a hotel room rather than flying all the way to Florida to escape your stalker and work on your book. Did you ever wonder why I made reservations for you in Cypress Bay? I wanted you to be in a place where you could also meet someone. So have a fling, Aylin. Have some fun for a change."

Leave it to her friend to be thinking about Aylin's love life in the middle of a crisis. If only Angeline knew she was having just as many problems here as she was at home. She had a brief twinge of guilt about not telling her. Aylin thought again whether the stalker found her, or if the incidences in Cypress Bay were only a coincidence.

"Why can't you finish your book and have a fling with the hot resort owner?" Angeline asked when Aylin remained quiet.

When she put it that way, she couldn't think of a reason, but...what if she fell for him? She was never one to have flings or one-night stands. That wasn't her. She'd get attached. Like when she went out with that one guy three years ago, who then left her after six months because he thought they were casual, when she thought they were getting serious. That one hurt a lot. She didn't know if she was able to do it again. Or if she would be the one to ultimately walk away.

"I don't see how I can do that since I'll be working most of the time and when I'm not writing, I'll be going around gathering more inspiration for my books. As a matter of fact, I'll be going into town tomorrow. I want to check it out and see if it's something that would work for my book."

Angeline sighed on the other end of the phone. "Just think about it, Aylin. Life can't always be about work. You deserve to have fun."

"I am having fun. Writing is fun for me. And don't talk to me about life not always being about work. You drag me all over the place at night and on the weekends, but you're as much of a workaholic as I am, Ang." Aylin wasn't about to let her friend get away with it, if Angeline wouldn't let her get away with it.

"Ok. You're right. But you still need to let loose a little. I still go out more than you do. Call me later and tell me about the town and how you're doing. And especially about your hot resort owner."

"He's not my hot resort owner," Aylin refuted half-heartedly.

She ended the call with Angeline and thought about what was fun for her. Writing was fun for her, but it was also work. Angeline meant well telling her to go out with Simon, but her friend didn't know how hard she took the last break up that apparently wasn't really a break up. She never told her how much that one hurt.

At the knock at the back door, Aylin peeked through the curtain on the back glass door. She started leaving them closed for more privacy since everything that had been happening. Seeing Simon with a police officer, she unlocked and opened the door for them.

"Aylin, this is my cousin, Luke. He's the county sheriff and is taking care of what's been going on at the cabin. He wanted a moment to talk with you," Simon said as they walked in.

"Sure, would you like to sit down?" she asked Luke.

"That would be fine," Luke replied.

Luke sat down in one chair, while Aylin took the other, feigning innocence when Simon gave her a withering look before sitting on the couch. She knew he would sit next to her if she sat there, and she didn't think she could be that close to him right now after that kiss. She was still trying to figure it out. Especially after the conversation she just had with Angeline.

"Did you learn anything new about who caused the damage?" she asked.

"No. Do you know of a reason anyone may want to vandalize a cabin you're staying in?"

Aylin still wasn't convinced that what had been happening lately was connected to her stalker at home. "No, I can't think of any."

Luke stared at her some more, but Aylin wasn't easily intimidated. She'd spoken to many types of people as part of her research for her books—from victims to serial killers and everyone in between—and a county sheriff wasn't someone who scared her. Instead, she stared stoically back at him.

"Do you have a blank piece of paper and pen available? I need a handwriting sample," Luke inquired.

Aylin watched him for another moment before responding. "Sure, let me go get it."

As she walked out of the room, she noticed Luke and Simon glance at each other. She wondered what that was all about. With a mental shrug, she grabbed a blank piece of paper and a pen from her bedroom, then walked back out into the living room. "What would you like me to write?"

"Your full name will be enough. Print and signature," the sheriff said.

Aylin nodded before placing the paper on the table between them and wrote. First, printing her name, then signing right below. She handed it over to him when she was done. The sheriff scanned it before standing. Simon stood right after his cousin.

"I'll let you know if we figure anything out."

"Sure," she said dryly as Luke and Simon walked out the door. As if she expected the sheriff to tell her anything specific about what he found.

Before completely walking away, Simon turned to her. "I'll pick you up tomorrow night for dinner, Aylin."

She didn't expect to have dinner with him, but gave him a curt nod in acceptance. Closing the door, she locked it and let the curtain fall back over the glass.

Well, hell! She was in trouble. Her heart was beating fast, and it wasn't from being questioned by the sheriff.

15

"She's lying about something, Simon," Luke said as soon as they left Aylin's cabin. "Or at the very least, holding something back."

"I don't think she's the one causing all the vandalism." Simon wouldn't believe she was involved, or that she faked anything going on for attention. He may have questioned her involvement earlier, but he never thought she wanted any of this to happen. "What would she achieve by lying to us?"

"Nothing. I don't think she's responsible. But she knows something that may explain why the vandalism is happening. Has something been going on where she lives?" Luke mused.

Simon remembered her changing the subject when he asked about her and her family. "Perhaps. Sometimes I think she wants to say something, but then changes the subject or glosses over it."

"I'll look into it. Where did she say she was from?"

"Philadelphia."

"If something happened up there, I'll find it," Luke vowed. "Now let's go talk to the neighbors."

They walked over to Chris Foster's cabin first. Simon noticed one of the blue planted pots was missing. Hmmm... guess it did come from this cabin, but he wasn't ready to accuse Mr. Foster of vandalism just because it matched the pot at Aylin's cabin. Even if the man seemed a little off.

Luke knocked on the door. They waited and when they received no reply, knocked again. After waiting for another couple of minutes, they realized he must be out and moved on to the cabin on the other side of Aylin's.

When they approached Deanna Irwin's cabin, Simon thought he heard raised voices and looked over at Luke.

Luke knocked on the door. "This is the sheriff. Open the door." The voices stopped abruptly, and they looked at each other again. Luke put his hand over his service weapon and nodded at Simon to take a step back.

A few moments later, the door opened, showing Ms. Irwin dressed in a skimpy nightgown and sheer robe. She had her right hand over her chest. "Sheriff and Mr. Kerrigan. My, isn't this a surprise," Deanna said, her voice low and breathy.

"Ms. Irwin, are you alright? Is there anyone here with you?" Luke asked, while attempting to look around her to see inside the cabin.

"Oh, I'm fine. I was watching some television and must have had it up too loud." She looked up at them, running the hand not on her chest up the door frame, posing in what some may think as seductive.

Simon was not one of them. Women like Deanna were everywhere. They wanted only one thing. To find a man who could give them money and status. Thankfully, Simon was not that man.

"Can we come in? I have some questions I would like to ask you about the vandalism that's been occurring at the cabin next door."

"Oh, that poor woman having to deal with those hooligans vandalizing her cabin. Yes, please come in. I'll be happy to help any way I can." Deanna Irwin took a small step back, barely letting them pass by her.

"May I look around first?"

"Of course, I'm so glad you are here to make sure I'm safe, Sheriff. And you, too, Mr. Kerrigan. Would either of you like a drink?"

They both declined and Luke searched the cabin, while Simon took a seat in a chair. Deanna draped herself on the sofa, leaning her upper body and left arm on the edge of the sofa, her legs tucked to the side, the robe left open, showing her nightgown.

When Luke came back into the room, she tapped the sofa cushion next to her, offering him a seat next to her. Instead, he also sat down in a chair. Disappointment flared in her eyes, quickly changing to concern once again.

"Ms. Irwin—"

"Deanna. Please call me Deanna."

"Can you tell me what you meant by Ms. Miller having to deal with those hooligans vandalizing her cabin?"

"Oh, I saw a bunch of kids walking around a few nights ago. I figured they were the ones who have been vandalizing her cabin."

"Have you seen or heard anything else?"

"No, I've been so worried that they would come back and do something to me or my cabin. Mr. Kerrigan, I would feel so bad if something horrible happened at your resort." The woman's overly sweet tone was grating on him. He couldn't stand fake people.

"Don't worry, nothing horrible is going to happen, Ms. Irwin. You're perfectly safe here," Simon assured her.

"I'm so relieved."

"If you could print and sign your full name for me on the back of this paper." Luke pulled out the paper Aylin gave him, folding it up to hide her name inside.

"Oh sure. I'm not a suspect, am I?"

"No. I need to eliminate everyone staying in the cabins. It's a basic procedure to rule out those around the scene," Luke told her.

Once she finished writing her name on the paper, they both stood and left the cabin.

"She's something else, isn't she," Luke said.

"Yeah, I realized with one visit that I'm done with fake women who try too hard." Simon felt extremely uncomfortable sitting there with Deanna Irwin, and he couldn't wait to see Aylin again. She was more down to earth and real.

"She is that. There was no way those voices we heard were coming from the television. She had two wine glasses on the table and the sliding door cracked open. And I found this while walking around her cabin." Luke took out another piece of paper showing different paint swatches and their names written next to them. Pulling out the other paper with Deanna Irwin's name, he put them side by side, showing two different handwriting samples.

"Whoever wrote that is not Deanna Irwin," Simon concluded.

"Yep. It looks like a man wrote this and I bet anything he was in the cabin when we heard the raised voices."

"Mr. Foster?"

"Could be," Luke replied.

That was as far as they got with their cabin investigation. They went back to Mr. Foster's cabin, but he still wasn't there— or he wasn't answering. They would need to try again later, Simon thought. But for now, he needed to get some sleep.

Saying goodbye to Luke, Simon walked back inside the resort through the back and to the secure door leading to his apartment. What was Aylin hiding from them? Was all the trouble something she brought with her from Philadelphia? Or was it kids like Ms. Irwin said? He didn't know what the answers were, but he knew if anyone could find out, it was Luke.

16

The next morning, Aylin woke up and got ready to visit the town around the resort. She was not only curious about the place where she was staying, but she also wanted to do some research and get the feel of a small town for her latest book.

The book wasn't set in Cypress Bay, specifically, but it would give her inspiration for the town she used, or at the very least give her some ideas for a new book. When she first checked in, the front desk clerk told her Cypress Bay's downtown had several blocks of shops, restaurants, and other businesses. Luckily, it was also within walking distance of the resort.

She figured getting out of the cabin for a while would be for the best today. After last night, she wasn't ready to see Simon again. Aylin knew he didn't buy that there wasn't anything else going on in her life. He'd probably continue to stare at her until she caved. His cousin didn't believe her either. She'd bet all she owned the sheriff knew what was going on back in Philadelphia before she even woke up this morning.

It was only a matter of time before Simon found out, too. And now that she thought about it, it was pretty ridiculous that she didn't tell them what was going on last night. She could have saved them all the headache of going around the issue, and dealt with it right then and there.

She also wanted to leave for the day because they were prepping outside the cabin today for repainting with the plan to do the paint job early the next morning. No way was she going to get any writing done when there were a bunch of people hanging around her cabin. She wanted to leave before they showed up.

Grabbing a backpack, she filled it with her wallet, phone, a brochure with a map of the town she picked up when she checked in to the resort, a small notebook, a pen, and a few other necessities. She walked out the front door and locked it before heading toward the resort. The main driveway in front of Cypress Bay Manor led to the downtown area. Knowing she would be away from her cabin, she was glad they cleaned up the paint; the steps dried enough for her to go out the front door so she could lock up the cabin. She definitely didn't want to leave the glass door unlocked while she was gone all day.

She took the map out as she walked. The resort was southwest of Cypress Bay's downtown, while the rest of downtown was in a grid pattern. That should make it easy to plan her day. She could walk straight up next to the lake, then walk up and down each of the streets, taking everything in.

There were several places she would like to check out, and she circled those on the brochure's map last night. An artisan shop, a tea and book shop—that should be interesting—and a sandwich shop where she could get some lunch were all locations she would stop by along the way.

As she walked through the town, Aylin stopped every once in a while to examine the unique buildings, going into a couple of stores at the edge of downtown, taking pictures with her phone, and making notes in her notebook.

When she arrived at the main central road, she stopped and took in the view. It felt like she had stepped back in time and was now viewing the quintessential small town. Buildings of all types lined the street as far as she could see. Some appeared European-styled with balconies and wrought iron banisters, while others looked like two-storied small homes surrounded with picket fences and wild gardens. They all had differing architecture and colors, and yet it all seemed to flow in a way that she couldn't imagine it any other way. Cars in tilted parking spots lined both sides of the street and there were posts with colorful business signs showing the direction of each location.

Aylin couldn't wait to explore! Snapping a few pictures, she imagined a new story set in a town like this one. What if one of the store owners was involved in something nefarious? Everyone thought the man running the small restaurant was kind and fair. But then they find out he ran some sort of drug activity or prostitution ring out of his second-story apartment above the restaurant.

Hmmm...she was thinking this could be her next book. She needed to go into some buildings to get a better feel for each of them.

Walking into the first store she circled on the brochure, Aylin noted it was simply named Artisan Crafts and Art. She immediately felt as though she was walking into a museum, but one that had shelves lined with beautiful pottery, paintings, and photographs hung on the walls, each with a discreet price tag hanging in the corners.

"Good morning! Welcome to Artisan Crafts and Art. Let me know if you have any questions," a woman called out from the side of the store, where she was arranging a few pieces of pottery on a shelf. Dressed in tan slacks and a form-fitting white buttoned shirt, she looked very chic and not what Aylin would imagine as small town fashion.

"I do actually. Where do you find all these beautiful pieces? They look like they belong in an art gallery or museum."

"Well, that is quite a compliment. Local artists do all our pieces. Most live right here in Cypress Bay and the surrounding areas, but we have some pieces from artists who live in Orlando and other parts of the state, too. Are you an artist?"

"Oh, no. I couldn't even draw a straight line. I'm a writer."

"So you are an artist! The written word is as much a work of art as a painting or a vase. You just do it with words instead."

"Thank you. That's a wonderful way of looking at it. Are you the owner?" Aylin asked, wanting to move the conversation away from herself.

"No, I like to keep myself busy, so I help," she said.

"Now, Amanda, don't sell yourself short," a woman admonished, walking from the back of the store. "Amanda is a tremendous help to me. I don't know what I would do without her. It doesn't hurt that I have an in with the owner of the building, either."

"Sharlene, stop it!" Amanda exclaimed with a laugh.

"Amanda and her husband own the building and probably most of the other buildings in the town. If you're looking for a place to rent, they are the best landlords ever."

"I'm only visiting and don't need a place. I'm actually staying in a cabin at the Cypress Bay Manor Resort."

"Oh! My nephew manages the resort. Maybe you've run into him. Simon Kerrigan?" Amanda asked.

"Um. Yes, I've met him. He's been helping me with the issues I've been having at my cabin." Aylin felt uncomfortable bringing up how else she knew Simon. No need to bring up that they were a little closer. Not that a kiss meant they were close, but—she also didn't know what it meant either, to be honest.

"You must be Ms. Miller then. I heard there was some vandalism at one cabin and that a writer was staying there."

"That's me, but please call me Aylin." She spoke with

Amanda and Sharlene a little more, directing the conversation to the items in the shop before making her excuses and leaving.

Aylin didn't expect to make small talk with Simon's aunt when she left her cabin this morning. It was a little more than uncomfortable. She decided it was a fluke and continued walking and looking around the stores. Deciding she was getting hungry, she spotted the deli sandwich shop she marked on her map and went inside to grab some lunch.

"Welcome to The Lunch Counter. What can I get for you?" the woman behind the counter asked.

The place was not very busy considering it appeared to have just opened a short time ago. Other than the woman who greeted her, there was one other person behind the counter, who was off to the side washing dishes.

"Hi. Yes, I'll have the roast beef on rye with a water please."

As the woman made her sandwich, Aylin thought the woman seemed familiar to her. Where had she seen her before? This was the first time she had been in town, so it must have been at the resort. It suddenly came to her, and that confused her even more.

"I hope you don't mind me saying, but you look a little like the woman I've seen every once in a while at the front desk at the Cypress Bay Manor Resort."

"That's probably my sister, Marinda. We aren't identical, but there are three of us girls, who all have similar features, so you may get a bit of déjà vu. Our other sister, Ryleigh, sometimes works over there, too. I'm Katia. Katia Kerrigan."

Aylin's eyes widened. One of the triplets! And holy cow, there really were a lot of Kerrigans in this town!

She finished her conversation with Katia, paid for her lunch, and sat down to eat. It appeared she couldn't go anywhere without running into them.

Finishing up her lunch, she waved and said goodbye to

Katia before opening the door and stepping out—and right into her cabin neighbor, Chris Foster.

"Oh, excuse me!" She wanted to take a step back, but the door to the deli shop was right there, closed behind her. Feeling uncomfortable with him that close to her, Aylin sidestepped away from Chris and then noticed he wasn't alone.

"Aylin, are you okay?" Deanna asked, coming out from behind Chris.

"Hi Deanna, Chris. Spending the day in town?" she asked, ignoring Deanna's question.

"Yes, I dragged Chris here with me when I couldn't find you in your cabin. Don't you just hate going to new places by yourself?"

"Actually, I prefer it."

"We were about to get something to eat. Care to join us?" the woman asked.

"No, I already ate, but enjoy your lunch. I have somewhere else I need to be, so I'll see you both later." Without giving them any time to say anything else, Aylin walked around them, giving Chris a wide berth. Heading in the direction Katia told her, she went in search of Hailee Kerrigan's tea and book shop, Leaf and Leaves. Of course, it was owned by another Kerrigan.

Not looking back, she kept on walking. She could feel Chris's eyes on her, though she didn't know if he was still looking at her or not. He gave her the creeps, just standing there, his arms crossed, not saying anything while staring at her.

She wouldn't be surprised if he were the one vandalizing her cabin. But that would mean one of two things. Either the vandalism wasn't connected to what was happening to her at home with her stalker, meaning it seemed she was a magnet for trouble. Or Chris was her stalker and followed her from home. That seemed unlikely. She couldn't imagine how anyone would know that she left or even the exact place she went.

Whatever the option, it seemed it was time to talk to Simon —and the Sheriff—about what had been going on at home.

———

Who does she think she is? Aylin fucking Miller.

She can walk around doing whatever she wants, writing things about me and my parents like she knows us.

She doesn't know us. She doesn't know me!

And then here she is, spying on me. Has she been following my parents, too?

The thoughts kept flowing, convinced Aylin knew more about them. Even after leaving the parental home—ha...that's a laugh...more like a hovel—at eighteen and not seeing them again, the thought of Aylin Miller following them was infuriating. They may even be dead. Who knew? But it didn't matter, she wouldn't use anyone in the family for her own gain ever again.

I bet she's been following me around the whole time I've been in Cypress Bay.

I'm going to make sure she pays for what she's done. She ruined my life and now I'm going to ruin hers.

<h1 style="text-align:center">17</h1>

Later that evening, Simon picked up Aylin at her cabin to go out to dinner. He told her he wanted to bring her somewhere other than the resort dining room, so he chose a small Italian restaurant nearby. It was close enough to walk, but he drove instead.

"So, what happened in town today?" Simon asked point blank as they walked down the path to Cypress Manor and the parking lot.

"How did you know something happened?" Aylin asked, looking at him, slightly alarmed.

"I only meant that I heard you ran into several of my family members. Did something else happen while you were in town?" he asked curiously.

"Oh, no—nothing. Really. But you're right. I ran into a bunch of your family. You weren't kidding when you said you had a lot of them," she said with a laugh.

Simon continued to stare at her, as though waiting for more. With a sigh, he gave up. Aylin would not tell him anything she didn't want to tell him. That much he already knew about her.

"There are a lot of us. What did you think about them and our downtown?"

"Well, I was a bit surprised, to be honest," she admitted as they got settled into his car.

"How so?" he asked once they were on their way.

"I wasn't expecting to run into your family, or for them to know about me. I know you said there were a lot of you, but I still didn't realize they would literally be everywhere I went. Especially with how many people were walking around town."

The conversation was put on hold as they arrived and entered the restaurant. Once seated, they gave their orders, and Aylin told Simon all about running into his aunt and cousins. How she enjoyed Hailee's tea and book shop, Leaf and Leaves. How Katia made the best sandwich she had eaten in a long time—and that was saying something since Philadelphia had some great delis. And how his Aunt Amanda was so nice to her, even though she felt uncomfortable speaking with her.

They lapsed into silence as the server delivered their food and while they ate. Aylin wondered if she should say anything about running into Chris and Deanna. Or if she should tell him about what happened to her at the apartment before she came to Cypress Bay. It wouldn't hurt anything to tell him about what happened in town. It was likely connected to the vandalism on her cabin. So he needed to hear about it.

As for the stalker at home, if his cousin was any kind of sheriff—and she was sure he was great at his job—he already knew what was going on. Asking for her name was for more than a handwriting sample to rule her out. She may only be a writer of crime fiction, but it didn't take a genius to figure out he was going to run a check on her. At this point, it probably made more sense to tell Simon what was going on.

Decision made, Aylin cleared her throat and said, "Actually, something did happen while I was in town."

Simon suddenly raised his head and looked up from his

meal, giving her a hard look. She stared back, not allowing him to intimidate her.

"When I left The Lunch Counter, I immediately walked into Chris Foster—I mean, I was walking out the door and Bam!—I literally bumped into him. He wouldn't move, so I shifted to my left to get away from him. Deanna Irwin was with him, standing behind him. I didn't see her until I stepped to the side. Deanna did all the talking while Chris stood there, staring at me. It was creepy."

"Did anything else that happened while you were there?"

"Not really, but later, after I left Hailee's shop, I felt like someone was watching me. It was that same creepy feeling, but when I looked around, I didn't see anyone."

"Luke and I haven't been able to talk to Chris yet. But I can let him know what happened in town. Maybe he can stop by to catch Chris at his cabin later."

"Actually, I think we need to call the sheriff and have him come over to my cabin. There's something else I need to tell you both. About why I'm in Florida."

Simon looked at her suspiciously. "Is this about whatever you've been holding back?"

"Yeah. And Luke probably already knows. I'm sure he did a background check after he took my handwriting sample."

"Do you always keep your head in your books?"

"What do you mean? Of course, I'm always thinking about my books. It's what I do," she said defensively.

"I meant you are as observant and knowledgeable of police procedure even when you're not writing."

"Well, it's not as if it takes a rocket scientist to figure out what he wanted to do with my full name." Why did what he said make her feel disgruntled and like she was missing out on her life? Just because she spent most of her time focusing on her books. That didn't mean she only thought about them.

She had a life. Okay, well, that life was mostly sitting in her apartment writing, until Angeline came over and dragged her out kicking and screaming. But she had a life, damn it!

"I'll text Luke." Simon took out his phone and started tapping away. "He said he'll be at the cabin in the morning. I can come by and meet you both there. In the meantime, I'll make sure you get back to your cabin safe and sound," he said.

Simon flagged down the server and paid for the check. They got up from the table and left the restaurant, and drove back to the resort. Once there, they walked in silence toward her cabin. The moon was bright in the sky, lighting their way down the wooded path. Aylin got that creepy feeling again. She stopped to look around but saw nothing.

"You alright?" he asked.

"Yeah. I felt that creepy feeling again. Probably still freaked out about this afternoon," she said before continuing to walk.

Simon observed the surrounding area before rejoining her. "I see nothing out of the ordinary, but now that you mention it, the hair on the back of my neck is standing to attention. Something isn't right."

Aylin didn't like that he felt it, too. That meant she wasn't only imagining it. Hopefully, Luke could shed some light on what was going on in the morning, she thought as Simon left her at her cabin.

Early the next morning, Luke and Simon knocked on her door. She wasn't much of a morning person, but she could barely sleep all night wondering how Simon and the sheriff would react to what was going on back at home.

"Hey, come in. If anyone wants coffee, there's some in the pot," she told them as she sat down on the sofa, picking up her own cup from the coffee table. They both went over to the kitchen and doctored up their coffee.

"Simon said you have something to tell us," Luke said. "Would this be about what was going on in Philadelphia and why you came to Cypress Bay?"

"Yes."

Luke sat down in a chair across from the couch, with Simon taking a seat next to her.

Simon spoke up first. "Just so you know, Aylin told me last night at dinner that she had a run-in with Chris Foster and Deanna Irwin. It made her uncomfortable."

"I can speak for myself," she said, glaring at Simon.

"By all means then," he said, making a hand gesture for her to continue. She quickly told Luke what she told Simon at dinner about her encounter.

"But that's not really why you need to be here. I'm sure by now you're already aware of what happened in Philadelphia," she said, directing her comment to the sheriff.

"Why don't you tell me what happened," he said calmly.

"I have a stalker."

18

She had a stalker.

Somehow it all made sense now, but he wondered how having a stalker in Philadelphia led to the cabin being vandalized. Did the stalker follow her? Or was she someone who attracted trouble wherever she went?

"Can you take me through the timeline of what happened?" Luke asked.

"You already know, so why do you need me to take you through it?" she asked, staring at Luke.

"I know the facts the Philadelphia police department gave me, not what you've experienced."

Simon watched Aylin absorb that and could tell when she gave in to answer Luke's question. She closed her eyes and took a deep breath before opening her eyes once again and began telling them what had been going on in Philadelphia.

"Someone broke into my apartment while I was out, destroyed a couple of rooms, and left a message on the wall."

"What was the message?" Simon asked.

"You will die for what you have done," she said flatly. "Of

course, I have no idea what the person thinks I've done to want to kill me."

"Could it have been someone who was unhappy with one of your books?" Luke asked.

"I don't see how it could be one of my books. I write crime fiction. Not true crime."

It shocked him what Aylin had been through as he listened to her and Luke continue to talk about the incident. He was even more shocked at his reaction to hearing she could have walked into her apartment with the stalker still there. Thank goodness her neighbor scared him off before she came home.

How could he care so much about someone he just met and had barely spent any time with? She wasn't even his type. And that was a lie he kept on telling himself. She was totally his type. He just didn't want her to be.

Simon was still struggling with wanting a family of his own, and at the same time, not wanting to get too close to someone in case he ever lost her. The fact he was feeling protective and scared for this particular woman's safety so strongly meant he needed to think about whether a relationship with her was worth the possibility of losing her.

Not that a relationship was something he thought about with her. She was a guest and not planning on staying in Cypress Bay. That wasn't conducive to building a relationship.

"Do we need to be worried that her stalker has followed her here to Cypress Bay?" Simon asked Luke.

"From what the Philadelphia police department says—no, we don't have anything to worry about. From what Aylin has told us—I say we can't rule anything out."

"But how could the stalker have followed me? The only people who knew I was coming down here are my best friend and editor, Angeline, and my parents."

"Maybe one of them accidentally let it slip that you were

coming here?" It wasn't impossible that a stalker could have found out where she was going. She already told them the flight and cabin were booked in her own name. It was also just as possible the vandalism had nothing to do with who was stalking her.

"You have a problem, no matter what. So let's go under the assumption that your stalker found you. You need to be more careful going places on your own. Don't open the door for anyone. Keep your cabin locked and change up your schedule from time to time." Luke laid out the guidelines while Aylin shook her head.

"That's not all going to work for me. I need to work, so I'll be here most of the time, but I need to take a few trips into town for research and supplies every once in a while. I don't plan those...it's whenever I'm ready for a break. I already have meals delivered when I remember to eat. And this one over here keeps dragging me out to eat at the resort," she said, pointing over at Simon.

"I can come around every once in a while to check out the area or send one of my deputies. Simon, can you make sure to send the same person to deliver food here?" At his nod, Luke continued, "That should prevent you from opening the door to anyone you don't know. Only answer the door for Simon, me, or the person Simon assigns to deliver your food."

"What if it's one of my neighbors or your many cousins? I think Hailee said she may stop by. Should I be worried she's my stalker?" she asked sarcastically. Aylin was trying his patience with that one. Mocking their ability to try to keep her safe.

"Do you think your safety is a joke?" Simon asked. Could she really not care about her own safety?

"No, of course not, but I'm also not stupid. I can make rational decisions as to who I should open the door for or not without being told who is acceptable to come in."

"Point taken," Luke conceded.

Couldn't she see he was worried about her? He didn't

want to control her. He didn't think she couldn't make decisions for herself. Instead, he was in awe of her strength—of how she had been continuing to go on despite a stalker breaking into her home and leaving her threatening messages.

"What about Deanna and Chris? If you looked me up, then you looked them up," Aylin said to Luke.

"You're right. Chris Foster is local. Not from Cypress Bay, but from the area. He has a history of anger issues, some that have landed him in jail a couple of times, though not for long."

"So there's a reason for why she feels creeped out around him then."

"It appears so. I didn't go too deep with him, but it seems that a surface check was enough. As for Deanna Irwin, I have far less than I'd like. It's like she was born a year ago. No prior arrests, driver's license was only issued last year in Ohio. But that's not surprising if she's stayed clean. I could do a deeper dive into her, but I would need to check some different channels if I thought she was more than a woman with an over-the-top personality."

"What you're saying is that if we go from the stalker finding me angle, it's most likely not these two. But that still doesn't rule out if it's not my stalker."

"And that's not something for you to figure out. Leave it to me and my deputies to investiga—" Luke was cut off by a loud bang outside. They all jumped up, and he walked toward the front door. "Both of you stay here."

Opening the door, Luke instantly saw what the commotion was and gestured them over. "Simon, you may want to come here and take care of this."

Simon walked over to the door, Aylin following him, where he saw his father surrounded by a ladder and paint supplies.

"Dad, what are you doing?"

"Hey! I thought I would bring out the supplies for

repainting the cabin. I told everyone else to not worry about it so they can work on other things."

A man in coveralls ran up and apologized to Simon. "We turned around for one moment to grab some other supplies and he took off with our cart."

"Dad, I'm so glad you're here. I was looking for you earlier to talk to you about something. Why don't we let Mike get started on the cabin and we can go to my office. You can come back later to help."

"Sure. That sounds good. Save me some of the painting, Mike," Simon's father said to the man, turning to walk back to the resort.

Simon told Aylin he would be back later that afternoon and asked Luke to keep him informed about any new information.

"Don't worry about this, Mike. Do what you need to paint the cabin. I'll take care of my father." Simon jogged over to his father to walk with him back to the resort.

19

After getting his father situated with a new job—one that he would hopefully stay at without wandering to "help" the other employees—Simon needed to process more than a few things. Making his way back to his office, he shut himself in.

Eyeing his desk covered in stacks of papers, files, and his laptop computer, he should get some paperwork done. Most people would look at him and think, "Oh, here's this guy who was handed a successful resort. I bet he walked around all day doing nothing."

But it was actually a lot of work running the resort. Growing up, he never realized how much paperwork or the need to manage every detail was involved. Each department had specific needs, inventory, and reports.

Yes, he had people in place who took care of each area, but he still had to frequently meet with the department managers to go over those needs, inventory, and reports. Then he made decisions based on those meetings. Just because a department manager said they needed a new employee, new linens, or a new bloody stove—thanks for that one, Oliver—didn't mean they got them or really needed them.

Right now, though, he couldn't think about any of it. Aylin had a stalker. He couldn't get it out of his mind. Who would want to hurt her? Was it related to her books? Or just some whacko who became fixated on her? Sighing, he thought they probably would never know.

Still, Simon worried her stalker was connected to the vandalism happening at her cabin. He wasn't sure how it would be connected, but something about it didn't seem right.

Was it Chris Foster? Luke said he had anger issues and often became violent. Aylin said she got a creepy feeling about him and after what she said happened in town, he wouldn't be surprised if he was involved. But the man was a local, so how could he be her stalker?

He also couldn't keep Aylin and the way he was feeling about her out of his mind. Simon could understand why someone would become fixated on her. He was on his way to becoming fixated himself. The sexual tension rose between them the more time they spent together. Simon wondered if she could feel it, too.

He would need to do something about it. The kiss they already shared was beyond scorching. If a kiss affected him that way, then he couldn't imagine how sex with her would make him feel.

There was still the issue of getting too involved. He would need to make sure to not become attached. Staying single was still the safest way to go for him. The last thing he wanted was to end up like his father—devastated and broken—a shell of a man.

A fling? Could he do it? That was a stupid question. Of course, he could do it. It wasn't like he'd been a saint. He even had some one-night stands a time or two. Outside Cypress Bay, of course. No need to worry about running into the woman daily when he wasn't planning on continuing a relationship with her. But could he have a fling with Aylin specifically and not get attached?

He wasn't so sure, and that was what had him so worried.

Simon would take it one day at a time while Aylin was at the resort. After all, she didn't live nearby and would go home soon. Even if he wanted a long-term relationship with Aylin—which he didn't—it would mean she would have to leave her home and move to Cypress Bay. He was tied to the resort and was in no position to move away.

Deep in thought, Simon didn't hear the door open or know that someone was standing in the doorway until the person cleared her throat. At the sound, he jumped a little, knocking off one of his paper stacks onto the floor.

At the throaty laugh, he looked up and noticed Aylin standing there, leaning against the doorjamb with her hands in her pockets. Seeing her with a smile on her face made him happy.

"Hello." Would he ever get used to seeing her? How would he feel when she was gone? No, now wasn't the time for that when she was standing right in front of him.

"Hi. I know you said you would come by later, but I couldn't work with all the people around the cabin painting. I thought I would come over and see..." Aylin began as she moved into the room, closing the door.

He got up out of his chair and walked over to meet Aylin in the center of his office. "See what?"

"See this." Aylin rose up on her toes, set one hand on his right shoulder, the other on his chest before pressing her lips to his. Licking the seam of her lips, he took over and plunged his tongue inside as soon as she opened her mouth.

Simon put his hands around her waist and tugged her closer before tilting his head to the side, taking the kiss deeper. Moving his hands down her sides, over her hips, buttocks, until wrapping his hands around the back of her thighs, he lifted

Aylin. She quickly wrapped her arms around his neck and her legs around his waist to keep steady. He loved the feel of her surrounding him.

Moaning into the kiss, he moved toward the door, pressing her against it so he would have more leverage to move his hands over her. He couldn't get enough of her taste. Clenching one hand into her hair just behind her head, as he continued to parry his tongue against hers.

Breaking the kiss, he nipped at her lower lip to her jaw until he reached below her ear. Giving her a tiny lick, he smiled as she moaned his name. "Simon."

He'd never considered having sex in his office, but he was seriously ten seconds away from shoving everything off his desk to lay her out over it. As he was considering this, someone knocked on the door, making them both jump.

Aylin quickly disentangled herself from Simon and eased away from the door, moving to stand by the chairs in front of his desk. He couldn't help noticing how her chest moved as she took in deep breaths. At the second knock, he opened the door to find Oliver.

Comfortable in his office, Oliver walked right in. "I wanted to let you know I just got word that one of my servers is planning to leave in a couple of..." he began until he noticed Aylin. "Oh, sorry. I didn't realize you had someone here."

"Oliver, this is Aylin Miller. She's staying with us in Cabin B. Aylin, this is my brother, Oliver," Simon said, introducing them.

"Hello, Ms. Miller," he greeted with a smirk.

"I'm pretty sure you can call me Aylin," she replied dryly.

Noticing Oliver was about to comment on what he saw, Simon interrupted his response. "Yes, we were about to go to lunch. Maybe we can continue this conversation tomorrow," he addressed Oliver with a long look. Simon knew what his brother was thinking. Anyone with eyes could see what they had been up to before he knocked.

Aylin was beautifully mussed up. Her hair was messy where he wrapped his hand in it. Her lips were pink and puffy. And she had red marks from his scruff on her jaw and neck. He probably looked quite disheveled, too, since she ran her hands through his hair and gave as good as he did with the kiss.

"Sure...no problem. Enjoy your, um, lunch," he said, chuckling as he left the office.

Leaving the door open, Simon walked over to Aylin. "Maybe we should go get that lunch."

"Yes," she agreed, clearing her throat. "I should freshen up first. By your brother's reaction, I have some things to fix before going into a public place," she said wryly.

"You look beautiful to me." At her scathing glance, he pointed to the far corner of the office. "That door leads to a half bath. Take your time."

"I'll be right out. Then we can have lunch and talk about what that was before your brother showed up," she tossed at him over her shoulder before closing the door to the bathroom.

A fling. It was only a fling. Simon kept repeating it in his head, knowing he would need to convince himself after that kiss.

20

Looking across the table at Simon, Aylin could not believe how quickly things heated up in his office. She went to see if the jumpy feelings she was having inside her happened every time she was near him or if it was a fluke. She hadn't planned on kissing him.

Once she arrived at his office, she lightly knocked on the door. When she didn't hear a response, she cracked open his door to check if he was inside. She found two things. First, Simon was sitting at his desk, staring at the paperwork in front of him. And second, she definitely still felt those butterflies in her stomach when looking at him.

Right then and there, she had decided she needed to kiss him again. She wondered if she would have the same reaction from him as she had the last time they kissed. Expecting a little spark, instead it was like walking into a fully involved fire. To say she felt singed was putting it mildly.

The knock at the door was like throwing water over them. She was resentful of the interruption, but it was probably a good thing his brother showed up when he did. The last thing she needed was to be having sex in Simon's office. But in a bed. That she wouldn't mind. She snorted at that thought.

Still, her reactions to Simon amazed her. She didn't act this way with men. Ever. Aylin was never the aggressor, or the one who would start any kind of sexual relationship. But with Simon, she felt like a new and improved Aylin, someone who could act on what she was feeling without reserve. So unlike her.

"You mentioned we should talk about what happened in my office," he said.

She swallowed at the thought of talking about it. She just got her body to calm down. But she needed to be an adult and do this. "So, was that normal for you?"

Now Simon was the one snorting. "Almost having sex in my office, being disturbed by my brother, or how it feels kissing you?"

"Now that you mention it, all of it." At the mention of almost having sex in his office, she imagined being draped across his desk, or bent over one of his chairs. Damn...being a writer gave her a good imagination, and it was making her hot all over. With all this inspiration, maybe she should change genres from crime fiction to erotica. She took a sip of her water to cool off.

"I have never, not once, thought about having sex in my office. Ever. But let me be clear. Given another minute, I was ready to spread you out over the paperwork on my desk, strip you down and explore every inch of your body."

Damn. Did she say singed? She was about to incinerate from the inside out. "Well...I guess it was a good thing your brother came by when he did or we would have given him a show."

"Indeed," he said with a smirk. "I would rather have you all to myself, with no interruptions. And in a bed would be preferable."

"That could be arranged." Where did this flirtatious Aylin

come from? She never did things like this. Most of the time, Angeline had to pry her out of her apartment to go out and mingle with other people. Her friend always complained that when they were out, Aylin would spend more time studying people rather than talking to them. This connection with Simon—she couldn't think of any other way to describe it—made her more at ease with him. Whenever he was around, she was drawn to him, like some tether was linking them together.

She had to remember that she wanted nothing serious, and couldn't let that link attach them permanently. There was no room in her life for a man right now. Besides, she didn't live in Cypress Bay and would be going home eventually. Instead, she'd think of this as an experiment. A way to become a different Aylin for a little while. Maybe she'd learn something for a future book. The femme fatale who used her wiles to ensnare the unsuspecting older gentleman.

"Perhaps," he agreed, breaking her out of her thoughts. "But first we should talk about where we see this going."

"I'm here for the summer—or at least until the police back home find my stalker—why can't it just be as simple as that?" She wondered why that felt wrong to her.

"Agreed. So Aylin, what do you think about a summer fling?" he asked.

"I think I can manage that with you. I still need to write. It's not like I'm going to be available all the time for sex. I know it appears I spend more time out of my cabin than in, but I actually am here to get some work done," she admonished.

"Look around you. I'll need to work during the day and some nights, too," he softly cautioned, his voice hardening. "This is my life, running the resort, and it takes up considerable time. But I will find the time to spend nights with you. Does that work with your writing schedule?"

He had a right to be peeved. It wasn't like he didn't have responsibilities. He probably had more than she did between the resort and his family. "Sure. How about you come over to my cabin tonight? That work for you?"

"I'll bring dinner."

"Actual dinner, or is that a euphemism for something else?" she asked. Did she mention she was bad at this?

Chuckling, he said, "Actual dinner. I want to spend time with you."

He wanted to spend time with her? The last time she checked, summer flings were more about sex than spending time with each other and getting to know someone. This complicated things even more. She would need to keep her heart locked up tight.

"Ok." Suddenly feeling shy, Aylin went back to eating her lunch before excusing herself to go back to work in her cabin. She couldn't wait until tonight, but she was also nervous. She hadn't been with anyone in a while, but she was more nervous about how she felt about Simon. Would sex change the way she felt, or would she be able to keep a part of herself separate?

She guessed she would know after tonight.

21

The next morning, Simon slowly woke up with Aylin wrapped around him. He needed to get up to go to work, but he didn't want to leave the softness and warmth of her in his arms. His first reaction was to question whether he made a mistake sleeping with her. The next reaction, dismissed the first. He couldn't seem to help himself from being happy about it all.

His mistake was letting his feelings for Aylin rise inside him. Sleeping with her meant he wouldn't be able to get her out of his mind or resist spending more time with her. This would not end well for him.

Untangling himself from Aylin, she stirred. She was so adorable when waking up. And sexy. Her hair all mussed up, her eyes slit open—as if she didn't know whether to wake up or stay asleep—and with a slight smirk of her mouth. Like she knew how she could make him stay for another round.

Not that it would take much. Waking up with her in his arms had him ready to go.

"Where are you going?" she asked sleepily. Aylin was definitely not a morning person.

"I need to go back to my apartment and change for work. I

have meetings this morning," he said with regret, already putting on the clothes he wore yesterday. "What do you have going on today?"

It surprised him he asked. It was something a man asked a woman he was having a relationship with—not a fling. Now that he thought about it, he wouldn't have even bothered telling a fling why he was leaving or what he was up to for the day. Something else to think about.

"I need to write some more," she said, waking up more fully and sitting up in bed, wrapping the sheet more securely around her. "I'm on a deadline and need to send my first draft to Angeline so she can do a developmental edit."

He remembered Aylin mentioning her friend, Angeline, before when they were talking about what happened to her in Philadelphia with Luke. "I thought Angeline was your best friend back home."

"She is, but she's also my editor. She does all of my edits and keeps me in check. That's how we met, actually. The publisher assigned her to me. I was a newly published author, and she was fresh out of college. I thought my work was the best thing ever because I published a book. Then Angeline happened," she chuckled.

"What happened?" He sat down on the edge of the bed, facing her and settling in for a story.

"She got all up in my face about how my latest book sucked and had no plot. Then she went on to say I was lucky my first book made it to publishing and if I was going to make it anywhere, I would need to let her have complete control over my editing and let her re-edit my first book for re-publication, too."

"How did that go? Because in the short time I've known you, you don't seem like someone who would take that." He thought back to when he first met her. She was standing at the front desk of his resort, complaining loudly to his front desk clerk.

"I didn't. I went right to my publisher and complained. He said Angeline was right and to suck it up," Aylin snorted. "So I let her work on my books and you know what? She was absolutely right. I became a better writer, my books were better, and she became my best friend. She knows me to my core and she won't let me get too wrapped up with anything that's not good for me. Professionally or personally. And I would do the same for her."

"I'm happy you have someone you can count on." He knew what it was like to have those special people in his life. He was lucky to have a large group of friends, most of them family members, but also a few who were as close as family. Other than his brother and cousins, he was very close to his friend, Joel Madris. He owned the boat tour company next to the resort on the lake. Now that he thought about it, he hadn't seen him in a while and wondered what was up with his friend.

"Yeah...she's been great. I miss her, but I had to come down here for a while," she said, giving a little laugh that didn't reach her eyes.

"And when everything gets cleared up at home?" Did he really want to hear her answer to that question? He knew what should happen at the end of the summer—she'd go back home. Then why did asking what she was going to do feel wrong?

"Then I go home and continue with my life there. While Angeline tries to pry me out of my apartment to talk to real people instead of the ones that live in my head," she said with a sad smile on her face.

He wondered if she felt it, too. That odd clutch in the heart whenever he thought about her leaving. No, he could not be falling for her. He could not have the type of relationship he always wanted growing up.

After his mother's death, after all the grief and pain, having a wife and family was too big of a risk for his heart. He didn't dare add that to his plate. What would happen to the resort if he was to find someone and then lost her?

He had to concentrate on his work. And if that meant he lived his life having flings and no genuine connection to someone else, then so be it. It was safer. He wouldn't risk going through what his father was going through.

Getting up off the bed, he finished gathering up his stuff. "I need to go, but why don't you come by later for a lunch break. Say around one o'clock?" It didn't need to be more complicated than that. Lunches, dinners, and sex. He could do that.

"Sure, I'll set an alarm so I don't work past lunch this time."

Simon stood next to the bed staring at her, crooking a finger to motion her forward. She smirked and sat up onto her knees, dropping the sheet and scooted right up to him. Her naked body pressed against his clothed one made him crazy. Intending to give her a quick kiss, it swiftly turned into them gripping each other tightly and giving in to the lust they had for each other.

Moving his hand, he cupped her, flicking a finger along her slit, and up to the nub that made her moan into his mouth. He couldn't get enough of her. Already wet, she made him want to ignore all his obligations, throw off his clothes, and take her again. Maybe for another few hours. Screw work!

But he couldn't do it. He held onto responsibility like a kid with a candy bar. Especially when it came to the family's resort.

He could, however, give Aylin an orgasm before he left. Give them both something to remember during the workday until they could have each other once again later tonight.

Dipping a finger inside, he flicked and rubbed her clit until her breathing sped up. "That's the way. Give me everything. I want to smell you on me all the way back to the resort. Feel your wetness on my hand and know I did that to you."

His finger slid over and in her faster and faster, while Aylin squeezed him in her arms, holding on, her head now slumped on his shoulder. Simon could feel her breath on his neck, sawing in and out as she got closer and closer to her orgasm.

"Simon," Aylin moaned as she came, slumping against him in exhaustion.

Really needing to go, he slowly released her from his grip and she eased back, where she retrieved the sheet and wrapped it around herself again before leaning back against the headboard. "Have a good day at work," she said breathlessly.

Bloody hell! He could barely get his legs to work and his erection was pressing painfully against his zipper, but he needed to leave. He backed away from the bed and said he would see her later before walking out of the room and cabin.

Once outside, he breathed in the morning air. It was stale and heavy with humidity already. Ahhh...gotta love Florida weather in the summer. Thankfully, he drove one of the golf carts over to the cabin, so the trip back to his apartment would be quick. He had things to do, after all.

It was what he needed right now. His work. He would think about Aylin and what he was feeling for her another time.

22

Feeling good after her night with Simon—and the orgasm he gave her as a morning goodbye—Aylin stretched out on her bed before rousing herself enough to get up and ready for her day. She really did need to work more on her book. She was behind. And not only because of what happened at home.

The incidents that occurred at the cabin also messed with her schedule. She hadn't been able to think much about writing, instead worrying about what happened and what may happen next. She thought the fact there were no new incidents would put her mind at ease, but it didn't. Who knew when the next one would occur.

Walking into the bathroom, she turned on the shower and grabbed her toothbrush, quickly brushing her teeth while she waited for the water to heat. It did so pretty fast she figured the cabin had a tankless water heater somewhere. The one in her apartment at home took forever, and so she had the habit of turning on the shower before doing anything else.

Finished with that task, Aylin walked into the shower, sighing when the heat warmed up her sore body. Simon knew what he was doing. She'd never had so many orgasms in one night before. Thinking back to last night made her flush all over.

Simon came to the cabin with dinner, like he said he would. She had kind of hoped they would have gone straight to bed—or the couch would have worked, too. Instead, he set down a warming bag and a cooler on the kitchen island counter, then asked her to take out some plates, wine glasses, and silverware. He pulled out a pan of some sort of pasta dish and bread from the warming bag, and some chilled white wine and individual salads from the cooler, setting them in the middle of the island.

Sitting at the small, intimate dining table, they talked about the rest of the day after the kiss in his office and lunch together. The sexual tension was palpable. But she kept on eating until they finished with the delicious meal.

Simon grabbed the wine and his wineglass, indicating they should move over to the living room. Placing the bottle and his glass on the coffee table, he sat down on the couch. She followed his lead, putting down her glass to sit on the couch next to him. But before she sat all the way down, he pulled her into his arms and turned her so her back was on the couch with him hovering over her.

"Now that's better," he murmured. His gaze on her full of desire.

It surprised her. She wasn't a hag or anything. But she was a no frills sort of girl who rarely wore makeup, and her hair was forever up in a ponytail to keep it out of her face while she was busy writing.

Aylin thought being the owner of a resort meant he may be the type of man to like a more sophisticated woman. One who wore makeup and dressed in something more girly than jeans and sneakers. Sure, she liked more feminine shirts, but she wasn't what others would call 'put together'.

"And now that you have me here, what do you plan on doing?" She was curious about how this would go. It wasn't like she was inexperienced, yet she also wasn't one to go out or sleep around a lot. Aylin was more curious because the kisses they shared previously were the hottest things she had ever experienced—so how was sex with him going to make her feel?

Whispered words about his plans incited a deep need inside her. "I'm going to start with your mouth. I didn't have enough of it this afternoon. When I've had enough—no, I take that back—I don't think I'll ever have enough. When I can't wait anymore how the rest of you tastes, I'll work my way down your body and lick, kiss, caress you all over."

She was going to lose her mind. There was no way she would survive what he wanted to do to her. No one had ever made her want someone as much as she wanted Simon and she was already wetter than she'd ever been before, with only the few sentences out of his mouth.

He set about kissing her, and it was even better than it was in his office. She was a melting pile of goo by the time he started working his way down her body, removing her shirt and bra as he licked, sucked, and nibbled on her neck. And the spot behind her ear that made her squirm. Oh, boy!

Her nipples were already peaked and tight before he even got to them. They tightened more when his tongue gave a soft lick to one, then the other, before he cupped her breasts in his hands and sucked her left nipple into his mouth. Crying out, she arched in pleasure, feeling it all the way into her core. He treated her right nipple the same way, eliciting another cry of pleasure from her.

But what really got to her was the dirty talk. He told her in detail how good she tasted and a play-by-play of what he was planning next. "I can't wait to find out how wet you are for me. I bet you taste delicious."

Kissing down her stomach, he unbuttoned her jeans, pulling them and her underwear down as he descended lower.

He kissed around her hip and down the outside of her right thigh, pushing her clothing off and throwing them to the side.

Spreading her wide, he placed her right leg at an angle; her knee up against the back of the couch. He gently moved her left leg, so her foot rested on the floor. And all the while, he was kissing and licking the inside of each leg as he moved them.

Resting his chest against the cushions, his shoulders pressed between her legs, keeping them open for him. His breath puffed out over her when he spread her out with his fingers. As he leaned forward and took a lick at her core, he moaned and sent vibrations throughout her.

Aylin couldn't stop herself from threading her fingers through his hair, gripping his head. That seemed to egg him on, quickly sucking her into his mouth while giving quick licks. Her mind was blank. All rational thought left, and all she was able to do was hold on and cry out in pleasure as her orgasm hit. "Simon!"

He slowly licked her down before climbing back up to give her a deep kiss. She could taste herself on his lips. It was a little sweet and musky and it turned her on more than she thought it would.

Picking Aylin up, Simon carried her into the bedroom and laid her down on the bed before removing his clothes. Taking a condom out of his pants pocket, he put it on, covering her again before swiftly thrusting inside. They both moaned at the contact.

And that first time was quick, but they had the entire night together. He got up to take care of the condom in the bathroom and came back to cuddle with her. They turned to each other one more time in the night, which was slower and more drawn out.

Aylin shouldn't complain after everything he did to her last night and the orgasm he gave her this morning. But she was actually a little disappointed he didn't stay for more this morning. She understood why he left, though. And if Aylin was being honest, she was glad he was gone for the day so she could process her feelings about him. Besides, she had her own work to do.

Already, she was falling for him. When he asked what she would do once the situation at home was no longer an issue, she told him she would go home and continue her life like she had before coming to Florida.

It was the truth. It was what she was always planning on doing. Stay out of the way for the summer, let the police at home investigate and try to find the stalker—or let the stalker figure out that she wasn't around anymore and move on—then go back home and live her life as usual.

So why did it feel like that was a lie? Why did she hope he would ask her to stay?

Shaking her head, Aylin got herself out of that line of thought. She was just missing Angeline, her parents, and home.

She'd only known Simon for a week. It was crazy to think they were having anything more than a summer fling. Not wanting to test how long the hot water would last, she finished her shower and prepared herself for the day.

She would spend the day getting back into her book, have lunch with Simon, then come back to write some more. She'd go with the flow and see what happened. Worst case scenario... Aylin would go back to Philadelphia and nurse a broken heart.

23

Over the next week, everything seemed to have calmed down, with no new incidents. Aylin had gotten a lot of work done on her latest book and she'd been spending more time with Simon, both at her cabin and in his apartment at the resort. They got into a routine where they would stay at one or the other's place for the night, then get ready for the day before going their separate ways to work until lunch.

Aylin would either go to the resort for lunch with Simon or he would bring lunch to her at the cabin—especially when he knew she got too involved in her writing sprints. Then they would go back to work and meet back up for dinner.

Today, Aylin was planning on spending some time with some of Simon's cousins—the Kerrigan triplets and Hailee—in town. Simon was going to come over later that night, where they would go out for dinner and then spend the night.

At the knock, Aylin peaked out the side window. Unlike what Simon first thought, she took her safety seriously. She wasn't about to open the door for just anyone, even when she knew who to expect.

Seeing it was Marinda, she opened the door. Since Marinda

worked at the resort, she told her she would come pick her up to meet with her sisters and Hailee at a downtown restaurant for lunch. Afterward, they would walk around the shops together before everyone needed to go back to work.

"Hi Marinda. Let me grab my purse and lock up." She walked over to the chair where she put her purse that morning, grabbing it and the cabin keys on her way out.

"This is going to be fun. I haven't spent much time lately with my sisters or Hailee. We've all been so busy," Marinda said, dressed comfortably in a pair of tan shorts, a tank top, and sandals. It was the first time she'd seen Marinda out of what she called her business professional clothes, of a straight-lined skirt and buttoned-up blouse.

"You all seem so close. I thought you would spend a lot of time together," Aylin said as she locked the door.

"Oh, we are close, but we also have demanding jobs and don't live together anymore. Though I do see Ryleigh more often when she comes over to the resort. Katia comes by every once in a while when she has someone watching the shop and brings by lunch for us to eat while we talk on my break.

Hailee's not around us a lot. She likes to keep to herself. But she was raised on her own with no siblings. We've always included her as much as possible so she would know what it was like to have them. But she's a bit more introverted than the rest of us and likes to keep her own company most of the time," Marinda explained as they walked toward her car in the resort parking lot.

"I've always wanted siblings, so I totally get it."

"Only child then?"

"Yes. And no cousins either. It has always just been me and my parents, who are also only children." Her grandparents died when she was little, so she didn't remember them at all.

Until Angeline entered her life. She never felt like she missed anything. But now that she saw how it was to have a big family and what it would be like growing up with siblings, she felt as though she missed out.

"Wow! No wonder you have that overwhelming look whenever you keep running into us Kerrigans," Marinda said. They were both laughing as they got into her car.

The drive to the restaurant only took them five minutes, and they were quickly ushered to a table, where the others were already sitting in a circular booth. They chose a Mexican restaurant with its brightly colored signs and decorations, Mariachi music playing in the background that gave it that quintessential interpretation of what Americans expect a Mexican restaurant to look and sound like.

"Drinking already?" Marinda asked, one of her eyebrows raised at her sisters. Flared out glasses of frothy drinks sat in front of each of the three girls.

"They're virgin, Mom," said the woman she assumed was Ryleigh, who was rolling her eyes at Marinda. "Hi, I don't think we've met yet. I'm Ryleigh. Heard about the trouble at your cabin and that Mike and his crew got everything fixed up."

"Hi, Ryleigh. It's nice to meet you," Aylin replied, greeting Katia and Hailee, who she met previously while in town. What she really wanted to understand was why Ryleigh called Marinda 'Mom', but the girls were already talking about what to order. "What's good here?"

"You can't go wrong with just about anything on the menu here. They have terrific fajitas, and their special burrito is so good," Katia said.

The server came by and they all put in their food orders, with Marinda and Aylin deciding the virgin drinks looked good, too. "Thanks, Carlos," Ryleigh said as the server left. "So Aylin. I heard you've been seeing our cousin, Simon."

"Ryleigh, leave her alone," Marinda chastised her sister. Ryleigh stuck her tongue out at Marinda and Katia shook her head, looking at them, while Hailee paid attention to her drink.

"It's ok, Marinda. It's not like it's a secret or anything. Sure, we've been seeing each other. But he's busy taking care of the resort. And I'm busy trying to work on my book."

"Maybe you can stay and make him not so busy," Katia said slyly.

"Oh no....no, no. I have to go back home at some point and deal with everything I left behind, plus my parents and best friend are there."

The girls appeared dejected at that, so Aylin moved the topic off her and onto something else. There was no way she wanted to discuss the summer fling with Simon with his cousins. Besides, she didn't want to risk them realizing she would love to stay with Simon. Sometimes she thought they were getting closer and their relationship was changing from being a fling to something more. But she didn't know what he thought about her.

"So Hailee, anything good come in lately?" she asked.

"Well, I know you aren't talking about tea since you said all you seem to drink is coffee when working. So for books, there are a few good options you might like in the last shipment. A new thriller from that author you mentioned finally arrived... Adrien Graham," Hailee said.

Her entire demeanor lit up when talking about tea or books. It was quite a change. Hailee seemed to usually spent a lot of her time by herself or observed rather than interacted with those around her.

Hailee and Aylin continued to talk about books, while the triplets were arguing about something quietly at the other end of the booth. She was trying to figure out what they were arguing about when their food was delivered.

"Don't worry about them," Hailee whispered to her. "Marinda and Ryleigh always argue, but Katia will play peacemaker and they'll get over it." By the looks on their faces, Aylin wasn't so sure this time.

An hour later, Aylin was ready to be rolled out of the restaurant. "Oh, my god! That was the best food I've had in a long time. I'm so stuffed there's no way I'm going to be able to eat dinner tonight."

"Let's go walk some of it off. We wouldn't want to be responsible for you not being able to eat dinner with Simon tonight," Ryleigh said with a wink.

"How did you know I'm having dinner with Simon?"

Marinda spoke up to answer, "I overheard him talking to Oliver, asking him to make something for you two tonight. I may have mentioned it to Ryleigh and Katia," she said, wincing.

"Ooohhh...a special dinner for two in his apartment," Ryleigh teased.

"Ryleigh," Marinda scolded, mouthing 'I'm sorry' to Aylin.

"Geez...I'm just joking around, Mom," the woman said, rolling her eyes at Marinda.

"Why do you call Marinda 'Mom'?"

"She's like a whole three minutes older than Katia and seven minutes older than me. She tends to mother hen us to death," Ryleigh complained, but didn't seem angry about it with the small smile on her face.

Katia just shrugged her shoulders. Aylin figured that might be part of their problem and why they seem to argue so much, but it wasn't her place to say anything.

The five of them paid for their meals before leaving the restaurant to walk around downtown. It really was a nice place to hang out. Aylin didn't even need to go into any shops to enjoy herself. Being around the other women was nice and something she rarely did in Philadelphia. Other than Angeline, she didn't have any other friends. Hazard of being in a solitary profession.

Hailee stayed with them for a little while, then said she had to go take over for one of her employees at Leaf and Leaves. "Bye, Aylin. Bye, MarKatRy," she said as she left.

"MarKatRy?" she asked the triplets once Hailee left.

"Yeah...it's something the cousins started a long time ago when we're all together. Easier than saying all our names," Katia explained, shrugging.

"It's ridiculous," Marinda complained.

"I think it's fun," Ryleigh countered.

After walking and exploring more of the shops and small museums with the girls, Katia said she also had to go to close out with her employees. Ryleigh had a job she wanted to check on in another part of town. So Marinda drove Aylin back to the resort.

"Have you given any thought to staying here?" Marinda asked as she parked.

"Umm...not really." Why wouldn't they leave this alone? There was no reason for her to stay. Besides, she just met Simon. Sure, she was spending an insane amount of time with him when they both weren't working. Yes, the sex was the best she'd ever had. But they would only have a summer fling. A couple more months and it would be over.

"I'm sure Simon will miss you. I know I will," Marinda said softly.

"There's always a way to stay in touch. And Simon will be fine. Our time together is only supposed to last until I need to go." Though Aylin was wondering why she couldn't stay. She could write anywhere.

But Simon wouldn't want her to stay and she wasn't someone who would move her entire life for a man. Nope, she definitely needed to go at the end of the summer.

24

Simon's days at work settled down considerably, with no more incidents at Aylin's cabin. His father had also settled in with the new job responsibilities they discussed a couple of weeks ago. That didn't mean there weren't still a few times he went off the rails and Simon needed to corral him away from trying to do too much or bother some of the other employees.

With his mother gone, he was happy to have his father around more. The one thing he had learned through the loss was to treasure every moment he had with his family—even if they sometimes were a pain in his arse.

And he thought of Aylin included as part of his family someday. Yes, he was still having doubts sometimes whether he wanted to risk losing someone he cared so deeply about. But he was also beginning to see he didn't have any choice in how he was feeling. He was getting attached to Aylin, and he was almost to the point where he wanted to ask her to stay.

Aylin was another reason for feeling better these days. Spending time with her in the evenings relaxed him in a way he hadn't in a long time. He didn't even realize he was so tense all the time until it wasn't there anymore.

With that thought, he saw his brother, Oliver, coming toward him with a scowl on his face. Even knowing some sort of trouble was brewing, he wasn't as tense as usual.

"Hey Oliver. I'm stopping by the kitchen soon for our meeting. I would have met you over there."

"Unfortunately, this couldn't wait. Dad is bothering my wait staff again. I redirected him by telling him I needed something fixed in the kitchen, but he can't keep on bugging my wait staff," Oliver growled.

Simon sighed. He knew things seemed to be going too well, and it was only a matter of time before their father needed to be talked to again. "I know. He's been doing so good, staying on track with the tasks we gave him, but I'll talk to him again."

"Thanks. Can we put off our meeting for another hour? I need to finish up the report I was working on before Dad showed up."

"Yeah...sure. But I'll go with you back to the kitchen and see if I can grab Dad for a minute."

Simon and Oliver walked to the kitchen. He wished his brother would take on more when it came to their father, but he was the one in charge of the resort, so it was his responsibility.

He had to admit that Oliver did a good job keeping their father occupied in the evenings, inviting him over to his house for dinner and stopping by their childhood home to help clean up. Simon couldn't be mad at him for not doing more at the resort. And Oliver ran the kitchen and all the dining areas. Which was something Simon didn't need to worry about or pay as much attention to, giving him more time to take care of other areas of the resort.

"Oliver, I'll have this fixed up in no time. The faucet just needed a new washer," John said from beneath the cabinet.

"Thanks, Dad. I'm glad you were here to fix it." And that right there was another reason he wasn't upset with Oliver.

Even when he pissed him off, he knew his brother would never take his own moodiness out on their father, who was still hurting.

"Hey Dad. When you're done, I may have some other things you can do, if you're interested," Simon told his father, John.

"Hi Simon. I'm happy to help. Give me another minute and I'll be right with you."

When John finished the repair, Simon led them out of the kitchen and they discussed some of the other things he could use some help with. If only he didn't witness how sad his father looked all the time. Just thinking about it reminded him of the loss, which was why he worked a lot. He guessed he wasn't so very different from his father in some ways.

Except he had someone right in front of him who helped when he wasn't working. If he gave himself a chance to build an actual relationship with her.

And while he wanted to build a relationship with Aylin, he was still scared of letting her into his life and then losing her. But she calmed him down like no one else and gave him an outlet to place his worries and concerns.

He could even admit that being with her had never felt like sex...it felt like making love. And now he was getting sappy. Shaking his head, Simon still needed to keep a part of his heart locked up tight to avoid getting hurt.

One thing no one could predict was when it was a person's time to go. What happened to his mother was proof of that. One moment she was with them and the next she was gone.

Enough morose thoughts!

Having cleared up most of his workday with some tasks he gave his father, Simon peered at the clock. Aylin should get back to her cabin soon after spending the day with his cousins.

Perhaps he should go over to the cabin a little early before they had dinner in his apartment. But before walking over, he had a few more tasks to do around the resort.

The lead housekeeper wanted him to look at the supplies list of items that needed to be replaced and the cleaning supplies they were running low on. The woman had never steered him wrong, so Simon knew the report would be accurate and he could tell her to put in the order.

Still, he needed to go over it first. One time, he barely glanced at it, told her it was fine, then had her reaming him out for an hour when he couldn't actually discuss the items she wanted to talk to him about. That was what he got for trying to go head-to-head with a woman who was at the resort when he was born. He quickly learned his lesson while his parents stood next to him, trying not to laugh.

Thankfully, it was early in his management career at the family resort. Having his parents—along with many of their long-time employees—around to guide him made Simon into the resort CEO that he was today. Someone who was capable and loved what he did.

Even knowing the woman's wrath was likely, he sped through the report, making a few notes. He was too antsy to take his time on it. Seeing Aylin was the only real thing on his mind. The quicker he could get to see her again, the better it would be for him.

25

Back at her cabin, Aylin called Angeline. She hadn't spoken to her in a while, and it felt like it had been forever. She was used to talking to her best friend almost every day. Looking at the call logs on her phone, she realized she hadn't talked to her for almost three days! Angeline called her and left messages, but Aylin kept getting involved in her work, Simon, or his cousins. She couldn't believe she never called her back.

"I thought you would never call me. You must be having a great time down in Florida," Angeline said, answering the phone.

"Sorry for not calling you back sooner. I've been working more on getting my book done," she admitted guiltily.

"Oh, I know you've been working. I have no doubt about that. But that's not what I'm talking about. Tell me what's been going on with that hunky man of yours." Angeline would never let her off the hook if she thought Aylin was finally having a life.

Aylin laughed, "Hunky man of mine? I don't know what you are talking about. And besides, how would you know, anyway? I haven't sent you any pictures of him."

136

"Ahhh...you are so hung up on him. Tell me everything!" she insisted.

"There's really not much to say. We hang out after he gets done working and after I'm done writing. We have dinner and talk and that's about it."

"Ok...I'm sure you're leaving out all the juicy stuff, but I'll let you pass for now. Mark my words, the next time you come back to Philadelphia, it will be to pack up all your shit to move down to Cypress Bay permanently."

This thought startled Aylin, causing her to raise her voice. "What! No way! Look, we're not even that serious. This is like a summer fling or something. I mean, the sex is great, and he puts up with my forgetfulness. We have a good time together, that's all it is."

Turning her head toward the living room, she thought she heard her front door close. Aylin hoped Simon came over early and walked over to the bedroom door, taking a peek around the small living room and kitchen area. Not seeing him, she decided she must have imagined it and walked back into the bedroom, settling herself onto the bed to continue the conversation with Angeline.

"I don't believe that for a minute. I know you, Aylin," Angeline admonished.

Aylin sighed. Did she want to admit to how she really felt about Simon? Angeline was one of the few people she trusted besides her parents. They were more like sisters than friends. And they told each other everything.

"You're right. To be honest, I do like him and I'm working on whether or not this would work. I can see a future with him. I'm just not sure if that's what he wants." After her last relationship —that wasn't a relationship—she wasn't sure she wanted to put herself out there again and set herself up for another round of a broken heart. Aylin could admit now that the last guy she 'dated' didn't hurt her as much as she knew Simon could if he ever left her.

"He'll want you. You're irresistible!"

"Haha...we'll see. I'm afraid of being hurt. I would have to be the one to uproot everything in my life to move down here. He has this resort. I'm the one with the profession where I can work from anywhere."

"What if you don't move for him, but move for yourself instead?"

"Maybe. I don't know, Ang. I need to think about it. I still have a couple of months down here to figure it out." She paused, hesitant to bring up what she really wanted to know. "Have you heard anything new about what is happening with my stalker?"

"No, it's been super quiet since you left. It's like they left when you did. But most likely they got scared off when your neighbor called the police on him and he almost got caught," Angeline told her. "Anything else happen to you down there?"

Aylin had finally given in and told Angeline about the incidents down in Florida at her cabin. Since Simon's cousin already contacted the Philadelphia police about them, it was only fair to update her best friend, too. Her friend was worried about her and telling her what was going on would help ease some of that worry.

"No, nothing else has happened. We're pretty sure it was just some kids fooling around and was a coincidence they picked my cabin each time."

"That's good to know. You'll let me know if anything else happens?" her friend inquired.

She knew better than to keep anything from Angeline. Her friend understood her better than anyone and was always aware when she held things back. "Of course!"

"So, what else has been going on lately? I've missed you so

much. When you move down there for good, I'll need to come visit you often," Angeline said slyly.

Aylin laughed at that. "I told you, I'm not sure if I'll be moving down here. But you'll be the first to know."

She was seriously considering it, though she wasn't sure she could put up with the heat. Of course, she did spend most of her time indoors writing. It was possible it wouldn't be so bad. She did like the area. The lake and downtown area were exactly what she needed. And if that also meant she would be near Simon, giving her the opportunity to see where that could go... all the better.

"Or the second. I'll be okay with that," she added.

"Or the second," Aylin agreed. Simon may be the first, if she was lucky.

Aylin spoke with Angeline a little more, telling her about her day with the triplets and Hailee. She described each of them, their businesses, and more about the town to her friend. After another hour of talking, she told Angeline she had to go.

Simon was supposed to be at the cabin soon to pick her up for dinner. Aylin felt comfortable enough to walk to the resort herself since there had been no new incidents, but he insisted on picking her up. She kind of liked it. But, of course, she would not tell him that.

Noticing the time, Aylin figured Simon would have been there already. He must have gotten tied up with work. This might be her opportunity to get him to stop working instead of the other way around. It couldn't hurt to walk over on her own.

She would just head to the resort and check for him in his office.

26

Excited to see Aylin, Simon logged off his computer, setting it to the side and plugging it in to recharge for tomorrow. That was another thing he'd recently changed. He used to pack up his laptop to bring back to his apartment with him to work in the evenings. Now he left it in his office, wanting to spend more time with her.

Of course, he sometimes sat in his office all night working. He spent too much time at work, but with Aylin, he found he wanted to be with her more.

And wanting more time with her, he walked to her cabin instead of taking the golf cart. Then they could walk back to the resort for dinner, holding her hand, having her near him, while they talked.

Arriving at the cabin, Simon let himself in with the skeleton keys the resort had for emergencies and to access rooms for cleaning. Most places were all electronic, but the resort prided itself on being more old-fashioned with keys to enter each room and cabin. There were positive and negative aspects to having keys over keycards. Regardless, it allowed him access to the cabin.

Aylin told him last week that he should come right in whenever he came by so he could stop her from working if she got too deep and forgot what time it was. Sure, he may be a little early. That just meant he had time to hang out in her living room until it was time to go. If he was lucky, she would be waiting for him, unless she was working or getting ready for their night together.

Quietly closing the door, he quickly realized Aylin was on the phone with someone, though he couldn't hear what she was saying. Sitting on her couch, he settled in, expecting to wait for a while until she finished with her call. Simon was about to pull out his phone when he heard her voice getting louder.

"What! No way! Look, we're not even that serious. This is like a summer fling or something. I mean, the sex is great, and he puts up with my forgetfulness. We have a good time together, that's all it is."

Rising from the couch, Simon clenched his jaw, his hands fisting at his sides. If that's what she thought about their relationship, then she didn't feel the same way he did. Not that they really talked about it, but he thought they had something that would go somewhere. That he finally found the person he would take the risk and pain of losing one day. Apparently not.

Not waiting to hear what else she was saying, Simon needed to leave before she was done with her call and realized he was in her cabin. He couldn't handle this right now. Maybe he never could.

Storming out of the cabin, Simon slammed the door behind him and headed back to the resort. He would get some more work done, or better yet, find his brother and cousins to go out to the pub downtown. He didn't want to go to The Tavern at the resort—she might find him and he wasn't ready to talk to her right now.

Yes, that was exactly what he needed. A little time to think things through with his brother and cousins. On his way back, he texted Oliver to meet him in the lobby, and told Luke and Noah to meet him at the pub.

Noah was Luke's identical twin. He was a doctor at the local clinic in town. While Luke went into the Army, Noah spent his time studying. It used to be hard to tell them apart, but since Luke bulked up while in the military, it made it easier. Noah was fit, but he didn't have the muscular build his brother did. There were a few other differences, like their hairstyles, too. Otherwise, they were identical in every way.

Oliver texted him right away saying that he would be ready in five. Luke and Noah said they were actually already at the resort to meet with Oliver and would also wait for him.

Walking into the resort, the three of them were standing in the lobby lounge talking and laughing at something Noah said. He thought the walk would help him calm down, but Simon felt more keyed up than when he left.

How could Aylin think they were nothing but a summer fling after all this time together? How dare she cheapen their relationship? Did everything they did together mean nothing to her?

Oliver noticed him first and walked over after saying something to Luke and Noah.

"Hey, I thought you were having dinner with Aylin. But we were already going to the pub and it would be great having you with us if your plans changed," Oliver told Simon.

"Oh, my plans changed. Let's go. I could use a beer," Simon scowled, already turning toward the door to leave. He had to get out of there and lose himself in something other than thoughts of Aylin.

"Wait a minute. Did something else happen? Where's Aylin?" Luke asked.

"No, nothing happened...no new vandalism. I just changed my plans and decided not to have dinner with Aylin tonight," he growled.

"I haven't met Aylin yet, but even I knew you were into someone. Now you're acting as though you wish you were never involved with her," Noah observed.

"You want to hear what's going on? I'll tell you what's going on. Let's go into my office. I don't need to broadcast my private life to everyone at the resort." He stalked off, knowing his brother and cousins would follow him.

Entering his office, Simon paced in front of his desk as the others came in, Luke coming in last and standing in the doorway, blocking most of the room from the hallway with his bulked up frame.

There was enough room in his office for everyone, but he didn't expect anyone to come by, so wasn't worried about the door not being closed. Besides, he was too pissed off to care.

"Okay. So let's start at the beginning. Why don't you tell us what happened with Aylin that makes you think things are not going well with her," Noah said.

Simon took a couple of deep breaths before he stopped pacing and faced the guys. "I went to her cabin a little early to pick her up for dinner. I figured we could spend some time together before heading back here to eat. But when I got there, she was on the phone with someone."

"What did she say?" Luke asked, narrowing his eyes at Simon.

"That we were having nothing more than a summer fling and weren't serious. She was actually quite emphatic in making that point to the person she was talking to." Just talking about it made his blood boil even more.

"I would like to point out that you did go into this as a summer fling. It is possible she wasn't aware that you wanted more."

"She knows," he insisted.

"Could there have been more to it? Maybe something you

missed...more of the conversation that you didn't hear," Oliver pointed out.

Could he have misinterpreted what she said? Taken her conversation out of context? Simon was too far gone in his head to work that out all the way. No, he heard what he heard.

"I didn't miss a thing. We're through. Apparently, we were never really together to begin with," Simon began saying. "You know what? I'm not even sure what I'm all upset about, anyway. I never wanted to get involved with anyone. The last thing I need in my life is a permanent relationship with some woman who attracts trouble and keeps me from my work."

At the gasp behind him, Luke quickly turned around and moved to the side, allowing Simon and the others to see Aylin standing there, looking like she was in shock. A look of hurt crossed her face before she turned and ran off down the hallway.

"Aylin."

"Now you've done it. You've just ruined the best thing that's ever happened to you. What are you going to do to fix it, hotshot?" Oliver taunted him.

Simon slumped down into the closest chair, his elbows on his knees, his hands clasped in his hair. "What have I done?" Taking a deep breath, he released all the anger and hurt he was feeling as he exhaled.

"You've screwed the pooch, Simon," Luke told him, staring him down.

"Seriously, Luke? Where do you get this from?" Noah admonished his brother.

Luke shrugged, not looking at his brother. "It's from The Right Stuff."

Noah shook his head and turned to Simon. "What are you going to do now?"

Recomposing himself, Simon stood up and fixed his

hair. "There's nothing I can do about it. It's probably for the best. Let's go to the pub."

"Nope. You're not bloody going anywhere but to make things right with Aylin. Don't let Mum's death scare you out of a relationship. We're leaving and you're finding Aylin," Oliver scolded him.

"Look who's talking about being scared. You're so locked up tight. Stone-cold, right?" he replied, taunting his brother back.

"Screw you!" Oliver turned and left the office. Noah and Luke each gave him a look of pity before following Oliver out, closing the door and leaving Simon in his office to himself.

"Fine! Leave! I can get my own drinks right here at The Tavern." Damn it! Now he not only hurt Aylin, but pissed off his brother, too. His cousins pitied him. And if he told himself the truth, he hurt himself, too, in the process.

What was he going to do now? How could he fix this? Did he want to fix it? Maybe it was for the best. She was leaving soon anyway. He needed to think, he thought to himself, as he continued to pace.

<h1 style="text-align:center">27</h1>

"The last thing I need in my life is a permanent relationship with some woman who attracts trouble and keeps me from my work."

Aylin couldn't believe what she heard. The men in Simon's office all turned around and she couldn't stand there anymore. If that was what he thought, then she was right all along. He didn't want anything permanent with her, and their relationship was only a summer fling.

Running off, she didn't know where she was going. She just needed to get away from him. Life would go on. She would stay in her cabin writing, getting food delivered from the kitchen, and never see him again for the rest of the time she was staying in Cypress Bay. It seemed she didn't need him after all. And if she really didn't need him, then why was this hurting so bad.

"Aylin, what's wrong?"

Realizing she was standing in the middle of the lobby lounge, Marinda was looking at her with concern from the front desk area. Wiping her hands over her eyes, she pulled them away, noticing they were wet from tears. "I just found out that something wasn't what I thought it was," she woodenly replied.

"Come on, let's go somewhere more private where we can talk." Marinda took hold of her waist, as though she thought she needed to support her, and turned her toward a room behind the lobby area.

It was a small break room with a couple of tables and chairs, a small couch, a fridge, and a counter that held a sink, a coffee pot, a toaster, and a microwave. Marinda directed her to the couch, and they both sat down.

"Tell me what happened," Marinda implored.

"Simon doesn't want me. He said I'm too much trouble and that I distract him from his work." Unable to hold it in anymore, Aylin crumbled against Marinda, sobbing uncontrollably.

"Was it possible you heard him wrong? Simon's hooked on you. One look at him and everyone can tell."

"N-n-no. Th-there was no mistake." Pulling herself together, she took the tissue Marinda handed her, wiping her eyes and face with it. "I must look like a wreck. I never cry like that."

"Let's go over to The Basin. I'll text Katia and Ryleigh to meet us. What you need right now is some more girl time."

The Basin was the poolside eatery, but she wasn't aware it was open in the evenings. Not that she had spent any time by the pool. "Oh, I'm not sure I'm up for that right now. Besides, we all just met for lunch and everyone said they had other plans for tonight."

"Girls' night overrules other plans. Especially ones that involve work."

"I don't want to interrupt any of your work plans." Aylin knew what it felt like to be interrupted in the middle of working. It could ruin a whole day and cause extra work later on when she would rather take a day off.

"You're not interrupting anything. Actually, we were all secretly hoping something would pull us away from the work we didn't want to do after that big lunch. So we should thank you for having trouble with Simon," she stated as a matter of fact.

"Well, you're welcome then," she said dryly. "Not that I'm having trouble with Simon," she quickly added. "We want different things. Apparently."

"Let's stop by the restroom real quick so you can splash some water on your face. You really do look a wreck," Marinda said with a small chuckle, most probably to lighten the mood. She appreciated someone who wasn't afraid to tell her the truth.

"Boy, you're just full of compliments all of a sudden," she said, trying not to laugh herself. She didn't feel like laughing, but her new friend was helping all the same.

After stopping by the restroom, Marinda and Aylin walked down to The Basin, a poolside eatery at the resort. She still felt upset, but knowing her new friends were making the time to be with her while she was struggling helped her a lot.

Together, they left the resort and walked down the path toward the poolside eatery. Aylin was worried they would run into Simon, but he was nowhere to be seen.

The Basin was a small building just outside the pool area with outdoor seating. When not in use, they rolled accordion doors over the ordering and serving windows to lock it up. Today, they were all open. The awnings unfurled over them to provide some shade on sunny days. As evening approached, there was still enough daylight left to need those shades, lights placed around the area for use at night.

She hadn't eaten at The Basin yet. But Aylin was told when she first arrived at the resort that while the kitchen from the resort's dining room provided food for the poolside eatery, it was mostly prep work with the actual meals cooked on site when ordered.

The menu at The Basin was what most would consider typical beach-side fare, like burgers, salads, and fries. But they also had a few specialities, such as the Mahi Mahi tacos and "build-your-own" rice bowls. And ice cream! Aylin was a sucker for ice cream. The way she was feeling, maybe she'd eat a gallon of it right now. Screw dinner!

Round tables scattered around the building, their umbrellas and chair cushions matched the deep red of the awnings, providing more shade and comfort for those eating.

The set up of the resort was in a straight line. The resort at the top, the pool and poolside dining in the middle, and in the distance was the lake with a dock and gazebo at the end. Manicured lawns lined with flower beds and trimmed bushes filled in between the areas. A path of crushed stone connected them all with benches strategically placed along the path to encourage guests to sit and relax along the way.

The pool itself was what she imagined an Olympic-sized pool would look like, but smaller. Not that she had ever seen an Olympic-sized pool, but it was rectangular and had lines painted on the bottom. She supposed that was for those who liked to do laps. At the moment, a group of kids played on the shallower end, and some adults were tossing a beach ball back and forth—as though they were playing volleyball without a net—in the deeper end.

Around the pool were chaise lounges and free-standing umbrellas in the same deep red. And around all of that was a fence with a gate to keep it all contained. A sign on the gate showing no food allowed beyond that point, though drinks it seemed were welcome.

Ordering a couple of ice cream sundaes, Marinda and Aylin grabbed a table. It wasn't long before Ryleigh and then Katia arrived. They also ordered ice cream sundaes and sat down to commiserate with Aylin.

"So I hear Simon's being a butthead," Ryleigh said after taking a huge bite of her sundae.

Aylin snorted, playing around with her ice cream more than eating it. "That's putting it mildly."

"Maybe if we tell you a little more about why Simon is reluctant to get involved, that will help," Katia offered.

Marinda picked up the conversation. "Simon has always wanted to settle down, find someone he would spend his life with and raise a family."

"Oh great...so you're saying it's just me he doesn't want? That makes me feel so much better," she said sarcastically.

"That's not what she's saying at all," Ryleigh said, coming to her sister's defense.

"Sorry." Aylin scooped up a big spoonful of ice cream and shoved it into her mouth. If it was full of ice cream, she wouldn't have to stick her foot in it anymore.

Continuing on, Marinda gave her a sympathetic look. "He always wanted what his parents had, and in some ways what he's seen with the relationships between his uncles and aunts."

"Not our family," Ryleigh muttered. "Owww," she yelled when Katia elbowed her hard in the side.

"Anyway, it was all he ever wanted. It was never a secret, and he made sure everyone in the family knew that he was hoping he would find the perfect woman for him to start a family with. But..." Marinda paused and then let out a deep breath. "When his mother, our Aunt Lauren, died suddenly in the accident earlier this year, he saw how much it hurt his father to lose the love of his life. Simon was hurting, too, but his father was inconsolable."

"It made Simon reconsider what he wanted," Ryleigh added.

"And Uncle John is still having a hard time adjusting to Aunt Lauren's death." Katia continued. "Every time he needs to redirect his father, it reminds Simon why he doesn't want to get into a relationship with anyone and risk losing her like his father lost his mother."

"He's confused. He still wants to find the woman to spend his life with and start a family. I still think he found it in you. But he also sees what his father is going through and wants to avoid the risk of future heartache," Marinda concluded.

"Look, I get all that. And I feel for him and what you all are going through over the death of a close family member. But you didn't hear him. It wasn't a matter of being confused. He doesn't want to be involved with me."

At that moment, Simon walked down the path, glanced over to their table, and met her eyes. With a frown, he abruptly turned and walked down another path toward the lake.

"See. I can't do this. I can't..." she bit out, the words barely able to exit without wanting to give in to giant sobs of grief. The tears built, pooling in her eyes before spilling down her face. Seeing him walk away like that gutted her. "I need to go." She quickly rose out of the chair and walked away before anyone else could say or do anything to stop her.

28

Simon wondered what he was thinking about getting involved with Aylin. Standing in his office would not make him wonder any less. Opening his office door, his evening front desk clerk, Tiffany, had her hand raised as though she was about to knock.

"Oh, you startled me!" Tiffany took a jump back when he flung the door open and was now looking at him wide-eyed.

"Sorry about that, Tiffany. What can I help you with?" See, he could remain professional even when what he really wanted to do was put his fist through a wall. Not that he would actually do it. He loved the resort and would do nothing to hurt it. Never mind what it would do to his hand.

"Um...well. I'm not sure if I should say anything, but I know how close you are with Ms. Miller. I thought you might want to know that she's in the break room with Marinda crying."

Damn. He may be feeling like his entire world ended—again—but he didn't want to hear that he made her cry. "Thank you for letting me know, Tiffany. Maybe just give her some time, okay?"

He intentionally left his response vague to make it appear Aylin was dealing with some sort of bad news or something rather than running out of his office after hearing him spout off nonsense.

And yes, he knew it was nonsense. Now. But he hurt. He still hurt when he thought about what she said on the phone in her cabin. Didn't mean he couldn't admit that he said things he shouldn't have when trying to blow off that hurt to his brother and cousins.

"Sure. I'll do that. I need to go back to the desk." Tiffany walked back down the hallway and disappeared around the corner.

Simon waited a moment, not wanting to run into anyone else, least of all Aylin. It may be possible to sneak through the lobby without her seeing him, but he didn't want to chance it. Instead, he turned left down the hallway, entered his passcode, and went through the door to another hallway leading to his apartment.

Entering, it was empty and flat, with no life to it. Compared to how Aylin's cabin felt, his apartment seemed more like a rental than the cabin did. No, he didn't want to be here either.

Walking back out of his apartment, he decided he needed to be around water. He would go to the pool, sit at the tables by The Basin and watch the guests enjoying his resort. And it gave him the bonus of watching the sunset over the lake later in the evening.

Decision made, Simon walked out his back door to avoid running into Aylin and around the resort to the path leading to the pool and poolside eatery. He loved the grounds of the resort and wished he had more time to enjoy them.

You found plenty of time when you were with Aylin. And look how well that worked out. No, he didn't need her to find time to spend outside. He would find the time on his own.

Arriving at The Basin, Simon spotted Katia first and thought how much he would like to spend some time with her. He didn't hang out with his cousins as much as he'd like.

Especially the girls. Roaming his eyes around the table, Marinda and Ryleigh were also with their sister. All the better!

Finally, his gaze landed on Aylin, their eyes meeting, stopping him mid-stride. He was not ready to talk to her. Seeing her reminded him of how much it hurt when he overheard what she said on the phone in her cabin.

Making a last-minute change in plans, he went to the dock over the lake instead. Simon didn't need to be around people right now. He needed some quiet, and it looked like the dock gazebo was empty. Abruptly turning away from the pool area, he made his way to the path going to the lake.

It was an asshole move, but it was what he needed. He'd been spending the last six months worried about everyone else. It was his turn now.

So why did he feel like he just made a huge mistake? Aylin looked as if she had been crying like Tiffany had said. And he could see how sad she seemed, even with the distance from the path to the table where she was sitting.

Arriving at the gazebo, he was relieved to find it as empty as it appeared from the pool. Leaning his arms on the railing, Simon stared blankly out at the lake. Boats littered the lake from Madris Boat and Lake Tours, the company his friend, Joel Madris, ran next to the resort. They often worked together to offer packages. Joel had several larger boats to take guests on tours of the lake, as well as smaller personal boats available to rent and take out on their own.

From behind him, footsteps pounded down the dock. Simon hoped he wouldn't need to make small talk with whomever was coming his way. He would do it, but he wasn't in the right frame of mind to do it for long.

"What in the hell are you doing?" Okay...that didn't sound like the guests he was expecting. Slowly turning around, the triplets were standing in front of him, glaring.

"Hey, MarKatRy!" Maybe if he pretended nothing was wrong, they'd leave him alone. "How are you doing?"

"Don't MarKatRy us!" Ryleigh growled.

"How could you do that to Aylin?" Katia asked, looking at him sadly.

"Why are you being such a jerk?" Marinda added in.

It looked like he would not catch a break after all. They were ganging up on him and it was never advisable to resist the trio when they were all together like this as a united front.

"I can explain," he started. Opening and closing his mouth a few times, he didn't know where to begin or why he should explain. But then he remembered how Aylin looked when he saw her and knew he had to say something to her new friends. "I didn't mean to hurt her, but she's the one who said it was only a summer fling."

"When did she say that? I've been with her this whole time, as she cried her eyes out over you!" Marinda stated.

He would need to come clean that he overheard her. "When she was talking on her phone at the cabin. I went to her cabin after she got back from lunch with you." He slumped his shoulders and leaned against the gazebo banister.

"Let me guess, then you decided to air out your frustration with what you overheard—which, by the way, was most likely taken out of context—destroying Aylin when she overheard you. You're an idiot." Ryleigh didn't pull any punches with him.

"You need to go after her," Katia told him. "She ran away after you left the pool."

"Fine," Simon grumbled. "But I'm still not convinced she wants nothing more than a summer fling." After the girls told him which direction she ran off in, he slowly began walking to find her.

He wasn't ready to talk to her, but maybe it all was a misunderstanding. He probably owed it to her to hear what she

was really saying to her friend on the phone call. And apologize
for what he said that made her cry.

156

29

Aylin needed to piece herself back together. The tears finally stopped the further she got from Simon, and she didn't want to break down again.

The last place she wanted to be right now was in her cabin, wallowing on her own—where others may try to come talk to her. She imagined the girls coming to check on her or seeking out Simon and sending him to her cabin to talk to her.

No, thank you!

A walk in the woods around the property may do her some good. There certainly were enough of them, with walking paths around the cabin areas and down to the lake. The resort probably had a good two to three miles of trails on this side of the property to walk. So that was what she would do until she felt better.

Now that she was away from the situation and a little calmer, Aylin understood a little clearer what was going on when she walked up to Simon's office. At the time, she didn't realize who was in his office, but now she recognized them as being Oliver, Luke, and another man she hadn't met before, but who looked a lot like Luke.

Must have been Luke's brother, Noah. The doctor. If it wasn't for all the muscles Luke had, it would be difficult to tell the two of them apart.

Simon had mentioned him during that first lunch they had together. It seemed like so long ago now.

So if they were all in his office, that meant Simon was venting for some reason. Why would he feel the need to vent to his brother and cousins about her? Everything was going fine between them. It seemed so sudden.

She stopped for a moment to gaze out over the lake through the trees on the path she was walking on. It was so peaceful here, away from the resort pool and so many people. It made her feel like she was far away from it all.

Not being able to think of why Simon would have cause to vent about her made Aylin angry.

What right does he have to complain about me keeping him from his work? I didn't make him take time off and spend it with me. He was actually the one who stopped me from working, so I would have the time to spend with him!

She walked down the trail some more, kicking small rocks and pine cones out of the way as she went. It was probably all working out for the best. Who needed him, anyway? Getting involved with Simon wasn't in her plans to begin with. It wasn't like she came to Florida hoping to meet a man who would sweep her away.

Aylin wrote crime fiction, not romance for cripes' sake! She should have kept to herself and not gotten involved. She was here to write, while the Philadelphia police took care of her stalker. Or at the very least, gave the stalker a hint that she wasn't around and he should give up and walk away.

That was assuming the stalker didn't follow her to Florida. She still wasn't convinced that what had happened at her cabin was because of her stalker from back home. Besides, there had been no trouble for a long time now. So apparently the person or people who vandalized her cabin twice were done. Most likely kids in the area egging each other on.

At the snap of a branch, Aylin stopped and looked around, waiting for another person to come around the corner. No one appeared. Was someone else on the path with her?

There...she heard another snap of a branch. Someone was walking in the woods next to the path rather than on it. Or it could be an animal.

She quickly tried to think about what types of animals would be in the area and couldn't think of any other than the squirrels regularly scurrying around. Maybe a deer. She had seen them around her cabin a couple of times, too.

Still hearing the branches snapping, she thought it sounded more like footsteps than an animal walking or scurrying around. "Hello. Is anyone else out here?" she called out. The sound of the footsteps stopped.

Aylin slapped herself on the forehead. *What am I doing? Apparently I haven't learned a thing from scary movies or the books I write.*

Okay, just because the sound stopped when she called out did not mean it was a person. She could have startled an animal, who was now sniffing the air to find out where the stupid human was located. Yeah...that's all it was.

The cabin was closer if she took the path on the left. The one on the right went to the lake, while the one straight ahead wrapped around the perimeter of the property. If she went left back to the cabin, then the animal would go on its way and she could take a nice hot bath to relax.

Yes, that sounded like a good plan.

Decision made, Aylin took one more look around. Not seeing anything, she turned and started walking toward where the path forked. She immediately started hearing footsteps in the branches again. No, that couldn't be an animal. Spinning around, she again peered into the woods surrounding her.

Then turned in a panic at another sound coming from the forked path.

Her heart sped up as someone burst out of the tree line nearest the path going to the lake. Aylin screamed, which startled the person, who was running with earbuds in her ears.

"Are you okay?" the woman asked, pulling out one of her earbuds. Breathing heavily, Aylin crouched down on her heels, her elbows on her knees and hands on her face, trying to calm herself down.

"Yes, I'm fine. I was just startled. I didn't see you on the path and thought I was out here alone," she replied, standing back up and showing the woman she was fine.

"Sorry about that," the woman said before putting her earbud back in and continuing on her run.

Though her heart was still racing, she felt much better now that she knew the footsteps she heard were from the runner. Walking once again, she thought she would really like that bath now. Aylin couldn't believe she let her imagination run wild like that. Yes, it was how she made her living, but her imagination was for her books—not real life.

But the footsteps you heard were not coming from in front of you where the runner came from, were they? So who was walking in the woods behind you?

That thought had her halting her steps. Maybe a quick jog to the cabin wouldn't be a bad idea after all. If ever there was a time to jog, this was it. Quickly looking around, Aylin saw nothing out of the ordinary, but in some areas, the trees and brush were dense.

Anyone could hide in there.

Turning back, Aylin walked quickly down the path to the cabins. Suddenly, a noise coming from the woods startled her, causing her to pick up her speed into a slow jog. A few strides in and the back of her head exploded in pain.

Aylin let out a scream as she dropped to the ground. Lying

on her side, a shadowed figure stood over her from behind, but she couldn't make out any of the person's features. Everything was blurry and hard to make out clearly. What happened?

"Help," she whispered. Why was she having such a hard time? It was like her body was not cooperating with her.

The man bent over...she thought to help her. Instead, he grabbed her by the legs in a firm grip, flipping her over, stomach side down. Sticks and other debris on the ground scraped across her body, face, and arms as he dragged her off the path into the woods.

No! This couldn't be happening. Why was she not able to grab onto anything? She had to get away.

The man dragged her further into the woods, the brush engulfing around her. Firmly hidden in the bushes, the man dropped her legs and began walking away.

Wait! Where are you going? Help me! Help...

Why couldn't he hear her? Was he going to help her? What was she doing lying around?

Aylin tried to make a noise...any noise. She couldn't seem to make her body do what she wanted it to do, nor could she remember why she was concerned with some person, anyway. It wasn't like she enjoyed spending time with people, she thought as her vision blurred and everything went dark.

30

Simon took his time following the path the girls told him to go down to find Aylin. He had to think about what he was going to say to her before he found her. Telling her he was sorry for making her cry should be first on that list.

Did that mean you are also sorry for what you said?

The voices of the girls in his head did nothing to ease his mind. They weren't even in front of him anymore and still they were getting on his case.

But they had a point. If that was a question they would ask, then Aylin would probably ask it, too.

Why did this have to be so hard? Couldn't he just find someone who would fit into his life with no drama?

Aylin does fit into your life and the bloody drama isn't her fault now, is it?

Great! Now he had Oliver's voice in his head. Why couldn't he have a family who didn't stick their noses into his life?

Simon moved over to the side as a woman jogged past him on the path. He stood for a moment watching her and wondered why he couldn't feel anything for her. He didn't get a good look at the woman, but he should have felt something for a woman who was obviously in shape and had a killer body.

Okay, okay. He let out a deep breath and admitted to himself that Aylin fit into his life. The drama surrounding her wasn't her fault. She didn't ask for any of it. And he could also admit that he was sorry for saying what he did that made her cry. He didn't actually believe that Aylin was nothing but trouble, nor that she was why he wasn't working so much. That was all on him.

Continuing to walk, he approached a fork in the path and wondered which way Aylin would have gone. If she wanted to sit by the lake, people watching without having to interact with them too much, then she would have taken the path to the right.

Thinking about how Aylin looked sitting by The Basin, her face full of hurt and the red-rimmed eyes; he figured she wouldn't want to be around other people.

So that left the path ahead of him, where she could wander around the property on her own, and the path to the left, leading back to her cabin and hibernation. His gaze switched between the two paths. Which would she choose?

He'd go to her cabin first. It was the shorter route and he could eliminate it quicker. If she wasn't at the cabin, then he would backtrack and go the other way. With a nod, Simon followed the path on the left toward the cabins.

Halfway there, he saw Aylin up ahead—at the end of the path before the turn to the cabins—half crawling, half dragging herself out of the woods and onto the path. What the bloody hell was she doing?

Moving closer to her, he called out, "Aylin."

This caught her attention, and she turned her head slowly to him, while trying to stand up. She stumbled, and that was when he saw the blood slowly running down the side of her face.

"Oh, my God! Aylin!" Simon rushed over to Aylin, pulling her into his arms and lowering her to the ground. "What happened? Did you fall?"

"Simon?" Aylin seemed disoriented and couldn't seem to keep her eyes open or on him. "What are you doing here? What's going on?"

"It looks like you hit your head. You need to go to the hospital." He was really panicking at seeing her like this. What if he hadn't come by when he did? Would someone else have found her? How long would she have been out here on her own, injured and hurting?

One thing he knew was that she wouldn't have been out in the woods or hurt if he hadn't been a dumbass. If she didn't hear him spouting off nonsense about her, then they would have been spending time together right now, having dinner. Instead, she was badly hurt. It was all his fault!

"No," she groaned while still trying to stand up.

Not liking that she was trying to move away from him, he scooped her up in his arms and carefully stood with her. "No, what, sweetheart?"

"No hospital. Cabin. So tired," Aylin murmured before passing out.

He'd take her to her cabin, but he would not agree to no hospital. He'd call Noah to come check her out. If he thought she needed to go to the hospital, then she was going. He didn't like that she was disoriented and lost consciousness. Add in the cut on her head that was still bleeding and the many other minor cuts and bruises he caught sight of on her face and arms. It was a miracle that he came around when he did.

Walking as quickly as possible without jostling her too much, Simon finally made his way to Aylin's cabin. That's when he realized he had another problem. He didn't have the master key for the cabin with him. It was in his office because he was not planning on ever needing it again.

He shifted Aylin to lean against the front of the cabin, still supporting her around her waist, and felt around her pockets to find her key. Locating it in her front left pocket, he pulled it out and swiftly unlocked the door before picking her up again, kicking the door closed with his foot. He gently placed her on the couch, not caring about the blood staining it, before calling Noah.

"Noah, are you still near the resort?" Simon asked when he answered.

"Yeah...we decided to stick around and have dinner here in case you continued to be a dumbass," Noah snorted.

He ignored Noah's snark and the laughter in the background. All that mattered was Aylin. "I need you at Aylin's cabin as quickly as possible. Bring your medical kit."

Noah's tone perked up at the other end of the call. "I'm heading for my car to get it right now. What happened?"

"I don't know. She must have fallen or something. Her head is bleeding. She's disoriented and passed out."

"I'll be there in five," he said and hung up.

Simon paced around the cabin feeling like five minutes was forever. A towel. He should get a towel to put under her head.

Getting a clean towel from the bathroom, he folded it over and placed it under the side of her head where she was bleeding. It would create pressure between her head and the couch, hopefully helping to stop the bleeding.

Standing, he couldn't stop himself from staring at Aylin. He couldn't lose her now. Even if she wasn't a part of his life, he wanted nothing to happen to her.

She said it was just a summer fling. That meant she would go home in a couple of months. He could live with that as long as she was all right. If she got better, he would let her go.

Please let her be okay.

At the knock, he opened the door to Noah, surprised but thankful Luke was also with him. Noah went immediately to

Aylin and examined her, occasionally pulling things out of his medical kit.

"What happened?" Luke asked, directing his attention away from Aylin and Noah.

"I don't know. She must have fallen or something. I found her crawling out of the woods onto the path. She tried to stand and turned when I called out to her. That's when I noticed the blood. When I got to her, she tried to talk, but then passed out," Simon recounted.

Noah butted in. "I don't like the look of this cut on the side of her head or that she hasn't woken up yet. Luke, call for an ambulance," he ordered his brother. "At a minimum, she's going to need stitches. I'd feel better if she gets checked out at the hospital. They'll be able to do more tests."

Luke pulled out his phone and called in for an ambulance. Simon looked on as Noah held a bunch of fresh gauze pads over the cut on her head.

"The ambulance should be here soon," Luke announced. "They'll bring a back board and carry her out to the main parking lot. The rougher terrain is too much for the stretcher."

Simon didn't care how they got her to the ambulance. He only hoped they would be quick about it. He had never been so scared in his life as he was in this moment.

31

Aylin slowly woke up. She was so tired she didn't even want to open her eyes. Maybe she would take a day for herself and just lounge in bed for a little while longer. Except this didn't feel like her bed at the cabin. And the persistent beeping sounds around her gave another clue she wasn't in the cabin.

Her head hurt like drums—an entire team of percussions—were beating inside of it and her body was sore all over, as if she'd been dragged around like a rag doll. Opening up her eyes into slits, she realized why it didn't feel like her bed. She was in the hospital.

She was startled to realize that she didn't remember what happened. Why would she be in the hospital? Panicking a little at the thought of not remembering, Aylin tried to think of the last thing she could remember.

She remembered sitting and talking with the girls, watching Simon walk toward them before turning away when he saw her, then her getting upset and running away.

Thinking about that made her want to cry, but she couldn't let herself fall apart until she figured out why she was in the hospital. She didn't know what happened after seeing Simon.

Where did she go? What happened to her? Did she fall? Why does her head hurt so much? And her whole body ached, like she had been in some sort of accident.

Out of the corner of her eyes, someone standing off to her right near the covered windows startled her. She twisted her head to look, then regretted the action when she felt dizzy and nauseous. Closing her eyes for a moment and keeping as still as possible, she waited until the feeling of nausea passed.

Aylin re-opened her eyes, trying to make out the person. Her vision was blurry, and it was difficult to focus on the person with his back to her. It was a man, that much she knew, and he was standing by the window looking out. She just made out that he was wearing a lab coat, so he must be her doctor? Trying to get a better view of his profile, she realized he looked like Luke. Exactly like Luke.

Why was Luke standing in her hospital room? No, Luke wouldn't be wearing a lab coat. And this man's hair was longer. Who was he? Why was there another person who looked like the sheriff?

She couldn't figure it out in her confused state. Hopefully, she wouldn't need to wait long before he told her who he was. And maybe he would explain why she couldn't seem to think clearly.

The man turned. "Good, you're awake. We were worried about you."

"Who are you and why do you look like Luke?" Aylin's mouth felt dry. She meant to ask in an accusatory way. Instead, it came out more like a croak.

Grabbing a pitcher of water and a cup, the man poured her some water, added a straw and held it out to her to sip before answering. "I'm Dr. Noah Kerrigan. I look like Luke because he's my identical twin brother. Or rather, he looks like me since I was born first, much to his dismay," Noah said with a quiet chuckle.

Noah gave her a little smile, put the cup down, and continued. "You're at the county hospital because of a head injury." Well, that explained why her head hurt. But why was the rest of her sore, too?

"Did I fall?" she asked.

"We don't know. Simon found you on the path going toward the cabins. You were trying to walk out of the woods. You seemed disoriented, had trouble standing and were bleeding from your head. Simon got to you as you were losing balance and about to fall. He said you passed out before he could ask if anything else was wrong or what happened. He brought you to your cabin and called me. After examining you, I decided we needed to call for an ambulance. I went with you in the ambulance and followed you through all your examinations and will continue as one of your doctors. You're also being treated by Dr. May. She's a neurosurgeon."

Aylin was having a hard time following everything he was telling her, but if she got it right, then she was on her way back to her cabin. She must have been on her way to it after she left the triplets. But why would she be off the path? And how did she hit her head?

"Do you remember anything about what happened?" Noah asked.

"No. The last thing I remember was eating with Marinda, Katia, and Ryleigh. I left, then I was here." Damn...her head hurt. Trying to think about what had happened made it worse.

"That's typical of head injuries and concussions. Of which you have both."

She didn't remember any of it. Walking in the woods, getting hurt, or seeing Simon. "How bad are my injuries and when can I go back to my cabin? I need to write. I'm already behind on my deadline," Aylin muttered. "Angeline is going to complain."

Noah told Aylin she was very lucky that her injuries were

not worse. "I won't go into all the details right now because with your head injury, you won't be able to process it all. Just know I will tell you all the details as soon as you are up for it. For now, you only need to know that you have a nasty cut on your head and a fractured skull.

"As for writing, you probably won't be doing any of it for a while. You would have a hard time concentrating or even staring at a computer screen until you heal from the head injury. And once you've been released, we recommend rest and relaxation—with a little physical and neurological therapy—until you no longer have any symptoms."

Aylin was not pleased and wanted to fight him on it, but she was too tired to even think about any of it right now. Her eyes felt so heavy and she was quickly running out of energy.

"Now you mentioned your friend, Angeline. Would you like us to call her or anyone else to tell them what happened?" he asked.

"No, don't call anyone. It would only worry them. They'll want to come down, and I'm not sure I can handle that right now. I'll tell them later." She knew Angeline would be on the first flight out if someone called her and said Aylin was in the hospital with a head injury.

It was going to be bad enough telling her once she was out of the hospital. Her friend would not be happy she didn't tell her right away. But she wasn't up for it now. The same went for her parents. They thought it was ridiculous to leave her home and fly to Florida when she could have stayed with Angeline or with them while the police figured out who broke in. This would prove their point.

He stared at her a bit too long for her liking, but then apparently went along with not calling anyone. "Okay, we won't call anyone yet. Simon is outside in the waiting room and would like to see you. He's been worried about you. Are you up for a visit?"

Her eyes filled with tears, but she willed them away. "I don't want to see Simon," she whispered.

Just hearing his name made her want to curl into a ball and cry her eyes out. Thinking about what he said hurt almost as bad as whatever landed her in the hospital.

Noah looked at her with sympathy. He must have been the other person in the office when she overheard Simon. Aylin thought he was the other person in the room, but hadn't been sure until now.

"Okay. Luke is also out in the waiting room and would like to ask you some questions about what happened."

"I don't mind seeing Luke, but I don't know what I can tell him since I can't remember anything."

"I'll send him in then."

After making sure she was comfortable and the water cup within reach, Noah left the room, leaving her to rest. She was so tired. Maybe she would just close her eyes and take a little nap.

32

Simon paced in the hospital waiting room and realized that his fears were coming true. Thank goodness he hadn't let himself become too attached to Aylin.

And that was a lie. Just the thought of her gets me through my day.

Shut up. You don't know what you're talking about. She's only someone I'm sleeping with. A summer fling.

But that didn't mean he couldn't be worried about her. She was still a guest at his resort. And they had a physical relationship. A very satisfying relationship that if he would finally admit to himself was not only physical.

Simon concluded that he may have gotten in deeper than he thought with Aylin. And that was really why he started spouting all that nonsense in his office about her. He was hurting after what he thought he heard from her phone conversation in the cabin and was just reacting to it in his own way. He understood now that he overreacted and may have taken her conversation out of context. If only he had kept his cool, admitted to overhear her, and then asked for an explanation.

Instead, she was in the hospital because he fucked up. His guilt was immense.

Luke sat in the waiting room, watching him pacing. "You should sit down."

He stayed at the scene where Aylin was hurt, coming to the hospital when he was done with his initial investigation. Simon knew Luke wanted to talk to her when she woke up.

It was something Simon was still torn up about. Did he want to see her for himself? Or would it be better if he pretended he was at the hospital to make sure a resort guest was alright after being injured on his property? Find out her condition, then leave.

"I'm good," he replied to Luke's request. "I've been sitting all day, it seems. I just need to walk." That was another lie. Other than some time this morning, he'd barely spent any time sitting at all today. He was thankful Luke didn't call him out on it. He had a canny way of knowing when someone was lying to him.

Noah walked in at that moment, and Simon stopped to look at him expectantly. "She's awake," he told them.

He let out a breath that he didn't realize he was holding. He felt like a ton of weight lifted from his chest.

"But that doesn't mean she's in the clear," Noah cautioned. "Let's sit down over here so I can tell you what's going on." They walked over to a set of chairs in the corner, away from some of the other people sitting in the waiting room.

Once they settled, Noah explained what was happening with Aylin. "Based on the injury on the back of her head, we first suspected a depressed skull fracture. It's exactly what it sounds like—the skull depressed in because of heavy trauma, which would have required surgery to correct. We were worried about the bruising or swelling of her brain, but so far, everything looks good. Instead, we determined she has sustained a linear skull fracture—where the skull bone broke, but is not moving—and a concussion. These are all correctable on their own with rest and some rehabilitation. She'll be at the hospital for a couple of days for observation before we release her."

Simon was relieved her condition wasn't worse. "So she'll be alright?"

Noah shook his head. "It's not as easy to answer that. Physically, she will most likely heal completely within a few weeks, as long as she follows protocol. Emotionally will be another story. Right now, she doesn't remember a single thing after leaving the girls. In her mind, she left MarKatRy and immediately was in the hospital."

"So the last thing she remembers is me leaving abruptly after seeing her." Simon rubbed his hands over his face in frustration. "What else?"

Noah continued his thought. "We still don't know what happened to her. If she does ever remember, who knows how it will affect her."

Simon perked up at that statement. "What do you mean if she remembers? Won't her memories come back when her head injury heals completely?"

"Not necessarily. Her memories can come back in an hour, years from now, or never."

Simon got up and started pacing again. He was worried about Aylin and what she might go through—now and in the future.

"I would like to go in and talk to her. I know she doesn't remember, but there's still a chance I can pick up some information she doesn't realize she has," Luke said to Noah.

Noah nodded. "She already agreed to talk to you."

"I want to see her, too. I need to make sure she knows I didn't mean what I said in the office and why I walked away." Simon was desperate to clear the air with her. Even if this was only a fling, Aylin had become more important to him than he realized.

"No."

"Excuse me?" He couldn't fathom that Noah just told him he couldn't go see Aylin.

"She doesn't want to see you." Putting up his hand when he noticed Simon ready to explode. "The last thoughts she has are about what happened with you. She is suffering from a concussion and head injury on top of it. Give her some time to heal before you go charging back into her life. You need to think about what's best for her, not to assuage your own guilt," he said softly.

That deflated him. Noah was right. He was thinking about how he felt guilty about his part leading up to her getting hurt instead of what she needed right now. "Can you tell her I'm sorry and I would like to see her to apologize in person when she's feeling better?"

"I can do that." Noah led Luke out of the waiting room, leaving Simon standing in the middle of it.

Without anything else to do at the hospital, he left to go back to the resort. He needed to think about how to make things right with Aylin.

33

A couple of weeks later, while continuing to heal from her ordeal, Aylin sequestered herself in the cabin, telling herself she needed to finish her book.

But mostly it was to make sure she didn't run into Simon. Aylin was afraid that once she saw him, she would forget the reasons she could not have a relationship with him.

Aylin was also afraid that if she left the cabin, she would be in danger again.

As her memory came back, she couldn't believe how lucky she was for her injuries to not be worse than they were—or that she was alive, for that matter. She spoke with Luke several times to relay bits and pieces of what she had remembered. The problem was, she still didn't really have anything concrete to tell him other than it was a man. She didn't get a good look at him and by the time she got her eyes on him, her vision was already pretty blurry and she was having a hard time concentrating.

Just the thought that someone wanted to hurt her made her shudder. Luke said he was going to do a more intensive background check on her cabin neighbors. Though she could not identify the man who hit her, she wouldn't be surprised if it was her neighbor, Chris Foster. He gave her the creeps every time he was around her.

She didn't understand why he wanted to check on her other neighbor, Deanna Irwin. She was as fake as a plastic tree, though so were a lot of other women who acted all sweet and sugary to get what they wanted. Usually a man or money. Deanna was a pain in the ass, but it wasn't a woman who attacked her. It was definitely a man. When she told Luke, he just said to let him do the investigating while she healed up and got better.

Whatever...he could look into whoever he wanted. What she wanted to do was write. Noah still wouldn't let her get onto her computer to work more on her writing. He said that after a little while on it, she wouldn't want to use it anyway after her eyes and head started hurting. He did, however, allow her time to write out what she wanted on paper—something about the hand/eye coordination being good for her to help her heal faster. She didn't know about all of that, but she wasn't about to argue with him.

Aylin wouldn't admit it to him or anyone, but her head was hurting, and she still had trouble focusing her eyes on even the notebook she was allowed to have, and all she really wanted to do was sleep. Instead, she kept all that to herself. No need for them to know and tell her to stop. Aylin was on a deadline and she'd already lost too much time because of some man who was hellbent on making her life miserable.

She did eventually contact her parents and Angeline. As expected, those calls didn't go over as well as she thought they would when she was still in the hospital. She guessed a head injury didn't make for good decisions.

Shocked, they wanted to come down right away to see her. She convinced them to stay where they were, downplaying that it was not that bad. She had already started to remember what happened when she called, but she told them she fell and hit her head, making it seem much less serious than it really was.

Still, Angeline knew better, but said they would talk about it when she was feeling better. That she wasn't about to browbeat someone with a head injury. Aylin gave in and allowed Noah and Luke to talk to Angeline, to tell her what actually happened, as long as Angeline promised not to come rushing down to Florida. She agreed and, while upset about what happened, admitted she was relieved Aylin had the help she needed.

At first, Noah had a nurse from the clinic come to stay with her at night. It was like still being in the hospital and after a while she was getting sick and tired of being woken up to have her blood pressure taken. After she complained, he asked her some questions—telling her to be honest with a stern look— examined her and decided she no longer needed the nurse at night hovering over her.

That didn't stop him from having someone always coming by to stay with her to make sure she followed the protocols set forth when she left the hospital. And she did still need someone to drive her to her appointments.

The girls came by frequently, too. She didn't know if it was because Noah asked them to or if they stopped by on their own. She liked to think it was a combination of both. Since Marinda worked at the resort, Aylin saw her the most. Katia and Ryleigh would stop in at the end of their days to check on her. Hailee brought her tea, saying it would help her relax and heal. She didn't know if she believed that. She was more of a coffee drinker, but it was nice having someone flitting around in her kitchen making her a pot of tea and sitting with her while she sipped it.

All of them would occasionally come by and stay the night, saying they were having a girls' night. Aylin knew it was less about enjoying time together and more about watching over her. But she kind of liked it. It reminded her of the girls' nights she had with Angeline.

Simon's brother, Oliver, delivered pre-made food to stock her fridge and freezer for her and anyone who was staying with her. It was delicious. He was a wonderful cook and even though she ate his food at the resort's dining room often; she had tasted nothing as delicious as what he was bringing to her cabin. He said he was working on a few new recipes and figured she was his captured audience to test them all out. If he was going to keep bringing her gourmet meals to eat, then she wasn't about to complain.

Even Simon's father, John, visited her. He had such sadness in his eyes. She knew from Simon that he had lost his wife suddenly. She couldn't imagine how that would feel. He mostly sat next to her, telling her stories about his wife. She thought it was just as much for him as it was for her.

The one person who had not come by was Simon. She was told that he was sorry for both what he said in his office and for walking away when he saw her at The Basin, but she didn't want to see him yet. She knew his family was keeping him away for her and Aylin was still on the fence whether she was ready to face him again.

Aylin missed him and was thinking he might be the one for her. The thought that he may not think the same of her hurt worse than her injuries. So she'd take some more time to heal and deal with what happened to her before deciding what to do about Simon.

If only they would also keep away her cabin neighbor, Deanna. She'd been wheedling her way in with some sort of food or fake caring since she got out of the hospital. It started to wear on her. She needed to tell everyone to stop letting her in. If she had to listen to her overdone, over-the-top 'caring' anymore, she'd scream. She didn't blame the guys for being susceptible to her. She just wished they would get a clue that the woman was playing them. Maybe she should say something. Having Deanna around was not helping her recovery.

Marinda walked out of her bedroom with another notebook for Aylin. This was the perfect person to move the woman along and relay the message to everyone else.

"Here you go. That should last you another ten minutes. I don't know how you can go through a notebook so fast," she said, handing over the notebook.

She shrugged. Aylin was always a fast writer and could go through pages and pages of notes within hours. "Marinda, would you do me another favor?" she asked, taking a peek toward the kitchen to make sure Deanna was not within earshot.

"Sure."

"Can you please get Deanna out of here? Permanently. And tell everyone else to not let her in anymore."

Marinda chuckled. "Getting on your nerves, huh?"

"Big time. I don't know how anyone can put up with her for more than a couple of minutes. She's driving me crazy with her fake attitude."

"I'll take care of it." Marinda walked over to the kitchen area to Deanna. "Ms. Irwin. Thank you so much for helping. We really appreciate how you came over to keep Aylin company."

"Oh, it was no trouble at all. I'm always willing to lend a hand anytime Aylin needs help. It's so scary to think about what could have happened to her out in those woods. If Mr. Kerrigan hadn't found her after her fall, who knows what could have happened to her." One thing they didn't tell her was that her injuries were not because of a fall. For some reason, Luke thought it best to keep that information known to only a few people. Namely Aylin, Angeline, the Kerrigans, and the sheriff's department.

"Yes, we're so thankful everything worked out, and she was

found quickly," Marinda concluded. "As I said, thank you very much for your help. Now that Aylin's feeling better, she's going to need more time on her own to get back to her life and work. I'm sure you would like to enjoy the rest of your vacation as well."

"Of course, but it's no hardship to help. Aylin, if you need anything, be sure to ask. Being next door, I can pop right over. I'll check on you in a couple of days."

"There's no need. Thanks for your help, Deanna." Aylin was trying to be polite, but it was getting harder to do with every word out of her mouth. With Deanna Irwin finally out of the cabin, she could breathe again. "Tell everyone she is not to make it over that threshold ever again, as long as I am here."

Chuckling, Marinda agreed before leaving to go to work. Aylin looked around and decided she had everything she needed to keep her busy for a few hours before others started showing up to 'take care' of her. Opening up the new notebook, she got back to work.

34

"No, the additional cabin plans should have been completed last week." Simon was going to blow a gasket if one more person didn't do the job he hired and paid them to do. "Right. You do that and call me back."

Hanging up the phone, he wiped his hands over his face and through his hair in frustration. He had to calm down. He was lashing out at others because he couldn't stop thinking about Aylin and what a screw up he was to hurt her.

Simon buried himself back into his work to stop thinking about Aylin. He spent all of his days either doing paperwork in his office, making sure his father was not getting into anything he wasn't supposed to at the resort, and looking at plans to expand the cabin area. He had kept himself so busy that thoughts about Aylin shouldn't even have a shot at getting through.

It wasn't working.

It was like she had a permanent spot in his mind that wouldn't go away. He wondered how she was doing, but couldn't bring himself to ask how she was or to go check on her. Everyone had been giving him dirty looks. It wasn't as though it was his fault he couldn't make things right. She was the one who had closed him out.

Then the rotation of his family started coming by to give him "updates".

"Don't you want to know how Aylin is doing?" Noah asked.

"No." It was better that way. If she wasn't doing well, that would make him more upset, knowing he couldn't make her better. If she was getting better, that meant she had decided what they had was not anything more than a fling. So best to just let it go.

"I'm going to tell you anyway," he said with a smirk, going through Aylin's progress and what she still needed to work on.

Bloody hell! It only made him want to check on Aylin even more to make sure she was doing what she was supposed to, so she got better.

It seemed as soon as Noah left, Luke stopped in, as though they had it timed. "Do you want to know the details of how Aylin got hurt?"

"There's no point," he answered, pretending to be absorbed in the work on his desk. "But now that you mention, it might be best to know since it occurred on the resort property. I need to be prepared in case we are going to be sued."

"Stop being an asshole, Simon."

He was being one, but until Aylin wanted to see him, he needed to protect himself. If she never wanted him around her again, then he needed to get her out of his system so he could move on. Luke told him that Aylin remembered what happened to her and then told him how she got hurt. This made him more alarmed and scared for her than ever before. To think someone came up from behind and did this to her was unbelievable to him.

Marinda, Katia, and Ryleigh came by individually and together. It was always scary when the triplets came at him together. As usual, whenever they were together, one would start reaming him out and the other two would pick it up, like a continuous round robin. Growing up with them, Simon was used to how they were together—it was even entertaining at times.

Though it was very disturbing, they were turning it onto him. Now that he thought about it, even individually one tended to pick up a topic and later another would continue it as though they were together the whole time. It was like they had a hive mind or something. They couldn't stop talking about spending time with Aylin, how sad she seemed and how she was doing.

Hailee stopped by, took one look at him, shook her head, and left. That was enough censure for one day. He'd had enough.

One by one by three, Simon told them all to go away. He needed to handle it his way. And his way was to keep himself apart from Aylin. Perhaps by doing that, he would start to feel better in another ten or twenty years—after she left to go home.

And who was he kidding? Aylin had him deep in his heart already. He was falling for her harder than he imagined. Simon didn't think he'd ever get over her in this lifetime or the next, if he believed in such a thing.

Putting his head in his hands, he rubbed them quickly over his face, then sat back in his chair. Still, there wasn't anything he could do about it if Aylin wanted nothing to do with him.

Looking at the clock, Simon noticed it was later than he usually left his office when he spent time with her. He figured he had two choices at this point. He could stay and immerse himself in more paperwork, or he could go up to his apartment and wallow for the rest of the night.

Heaving out a big breath, his only real option was to continue working. Especially since he had gotten little of it done in the last few days. All of his thoughts were on Aylin and when she might be ready to talk to him again.

Truth be told, he was eager to see her. Not that he would tell anyone in his family. That she refused him was killing him.

Turning back to his paperwork, he let out another breath. His resort was important, too. If she didn't want him around yet, then he would continue to work at what he loved until she was ready.

At this moment, it was dealing with the addition of a couple of new cabins. And perhaps coming up with names for the cabins would be better than naming them A, B, C, D, and E. It was another reason he wanted Aylin with him. As a writer, she was much better at coming up with names than he was.

Determined to not let his mind wander to Aylin any longer, Simon forced himself to focus on the cabin plans in front of him. The new cabins needed a back door. With a lock in case the front door could not be accessed, just like when Aylin's cabin had paint all over it.

He threw down his pen. It was hopeless. Everything reminded him of her, and that meant he would not be getting any more work done tonight. Rolling up the cabin plans, he secured them with a rubber band and set them aside. He logged off his computer and left it on his desk before walking out of his office and headed to his apartment.

The only thing he would get done tonight was wallowing on his own.

35

"Damn it!" Aylin threw her notebook across the room. "I am so tired of sitting around this cabin wasting away!" Maybe she should go back home. At least then she would be comfortable in her own apartment. And it couldn't be any more dangerous than it was here. Seriously, she'd been having more problems here than with her stalker at home!

Noah and Luke looked over at her with identical expressions of amusement on their faces and one eyebrow raised, mirroring each other.

"How do you do that?" she asked.

"Do what?" they answered together.

"Aaaaaah," she screamed. "Never mind, it's obviously a twin thing. Marinda, Katia, and Ryleigh do it, too. But it's just weird when you both look so much alike."

They looked at each other and smiled. She bet they knew exactly what they were doing. "So, what's on the agenda today? Any more torture—I mean wonderful activities—to get me back to normal?"

Noah ignored her snark. "Not much today. I'll have you work on the bike for about 30 minutes of light exercise. You're actually showing remarkable progress for someone with a head injury after only a couple of weeks."

The stationary bike had shown up at her cabin door the day after Noah had told her she was ready to start some light exercise a week ago. At first she thought he had brought it from the clinic or his home, but he told her he arranged for it to be brought from the resort's fitness room.

"Enough to let me get back into my normal routine and onto my computer again?"

"We'll see." Every time she asked, he gave the same response. She rolled her eyes at him and he laughed, probably enjoying their frequent banter. In all honesty, she was really enjoying it, too. She'd spent a lot of time with the Kerrigan family these last two weeks in her cabin. And they were beginning to feel like family to her.

Getting up from the couch, where she felt like she had spent an eternity, Aylin walked over to the bike and got on. She waited while Noah adjusted the tension and programmed in what he wanted her to do. When he was done, she started her slow cycling.

"You know. There is another thing you could do to decrease your recovery time," Noah said, not looking at her. He seemed to be awfully busy staring at Luke.

"Oh, yeah...what's that? You know I'll do anything to get back to my regular routine."

Luke gave him a nod before he answered. "Go talk to Simon."

Muttering a curse, Aylin moved to press the pause button on the bike. Noah stayed her hand before she could press it and continued. "Keep pedaling and listen. You're both miserable. And being miserable is not helping your recovery. You need to talk to him and let it all out."

She snorted at that. "Yeah, nice try, but I don't think talking to him right now is in my best interest."

"You would be safer if Simon was around," Luke piped up.

She thought that was funny, since she had more people around her than she ever had before. "I don't see how. The cabin has more people coming and going than a train station."

Luke looked frustrated. "We're all not going to be hanging around twenty-four seven forever. We're already tapering off how long you need someone with you because of your injuries. If you and Simon would get off your asses and work this shit out, you would spend more time with him, especially at night when you're sleeping and more vulnerable," he growled at her.

Aylin was getting angry now at how much they were pushing her to talk to Simon. "I know the only reason you're all here is because I was injured and needed help. And I appreciate it. But I do not need a man sleeping with me so he can take care of me."

Luke muttered something under his breath that she thought sounded like "stubborn asses." But she couldn't be sure. "Look, I appreciate all the help everyone has been giving me more than you all know. And I understand your concern about me, but I'm not willing to talk to him just to appease others."

"We don't know who hurt you yet, Aylin. You could still be in danger," Luke said.

"I know, but I've never been one to let someone else stop me from living my life. I may not be able to live it the way I want right now until everything is cleared up, but I still have the right to decide some of it."

They were both quiet after that as she finished up her exercise. Noah went through a few more activities with her, then left her to rest. She didn't feel like she needed to sleep as much as when she first came home from the hospital, though a nap sounded good to her now.

After a short nap, Katia and Hailee came over to eat dinner with her. She felt better than she did this afternoon. She really hated being cooped up, which was kind of funny to her since most of the time she secluded herself on purpose to write.

Angeline would laugh at her if she realized how much Aylin wanted to go out right now. Of course, she understood why she couldn't. She was still recovering from the head injury, though her head wasn't pounding nearly as much as it was when she was first hurt.

Noah told her that even if she started feeling better, she needed to take it easy and start getting back into her normal routine slowly to make sure she didn't have any lingering issues.

And of course, the other reason she couldn't go out right now was because Luke still hadn't found the person responsible for hitting her and leaving her out in the middle of the woods. She shuddered, thinking about what had happened. She almost wished she still couldn't remember. But it would be something that stuck with her for a long time. She also knew Luke was doing everything he could to find and apprehend the person responsible.

"Here we go. I can't wait until Oliver adds this to the resort's menu." Katia set out three dishes of a flaky white fish with some sort of creamy sauce on top, resting on a bed of brown rice, with a side of asparagus.

Hailee set out glasses of her homemade iced tea. "I know. It's so good. I'm not sure what's in the sauce, but he should bottle it up."

"I guess it's one plus of being injured here. Otherwise, I may have been back home by the time he started serving this at the resort," Aylin said.

They started eating their meals in silence until Katia cleared her throat and began talking. "You know...you don't need to go back home. You could always stay here. Maybe find a place to live. Or you could continue living at the resort. Make up with Simon, live with him," she said offhandedly.

Aylin put down the glass of tea she was just drinking and stared at Katia. She could see Hailee in her periphery, looking back and forth between them, as though caught in a conversation she didn't want to be in. "Sure, I can live anywhere I want since my job isn't tied to one specific location. But making up with Simon and living with him is a long shot that will never happen."

"It can happen. He's been a jerk since you got hurt. He is snapping at people or hiding himself away in his office."

"That's not my problem. He hurt me, Katia. I'm not sure I can get past that."

"It was all a misunderstanding," Hailee whispered.

"What?" she asked, turning her head to face Hailee.

"Simon came by early when he was supposed to meet you for dinner and overheard part of your conversation with whoever you were talking to on the phone," Hailee explained.

Trying to think back to the day everything went wrong, she remembered talking to Angeline that afternoon. "Oh, my gosh. What did he hear?"

Katia picked up the conversation. "You said what you had with him was only a summer fling and nothing serious."

"Yes, I said that, but it was only a piece of what I said. If he stayed longer, he would have heard me say that I really did like him and was trying to work out what I wanted to do about it. I thought I could move here and see what happened." Damn it! Why did he have to walk in and overhear her conversation at that exact time? Wait...how did they know what she said?

"Does everyone know what happened?"

"Well, not at first. I suppose the guys knew because they were all in his office when Simon was venting. Marinda, Ryleigh and I found out after you left The Basin. We talked about how to tell you with Hailee after you were hurt. We didn't think it was wise to talk to you about it while you were recuperating. So we swore the guys to secrecy until you were well enough to hear it."

"So what you're saying is today was the day when all the gloves came off," she said wryly.

"Yep!" Katia was too perky for her right now. Hailee was just sitting back in the chair, staring at her as though she was making sure she didn't need someone to hold Aylin up or something.

"Okay, I'll think about it. But what he said still hurt. I'm not sure I'm ready to talk to him or forgive him yet." Even if it was a misunderstanding, he never should have said the things that he did. They said he loved her, but she thought that was wishful thinking on their parts.

After Katia and Hailee left, Aylin decided she needed to talk to the one person who would tell it like it was with her. When Angeline answered, she told her everything. What Noah and Luke said earlier that day, what she learned from Katia and Hailee, and especially her hesitation to put her heart at risk.

"Aylin, I understand why you're confused. But you need to get your ass out of your cabin and go fix things with Simon. What are you thinking, throwing away a chance at a great relationship over stupid shit and flimsy excuses?" Did Aylin mention Angeline would tell her like it was or what? Even with her straightforward conversation, Aylin still wasn't confident enough about what Simon felt. Was she willing to take the risk after everything she heard?

"What if I decide I want Simon and to stay here, but he doesn't want me anymore? What if he doesn't love me? And most importantly, what am I going to do without you?" She was going to really miss seeing her friend every day if she moved down to Florida permanently.

"You can't find out until you actually do something about it. Love is about risks. If you don't put yourself out there, then you'll always wonder if you threw something great away. And if he does, I'll fly down to kick his sorry ass and welcome you home with gallons of ice cream and a shoulder to cry on.

"As for what you'll do without me? Probably fall into a deep depression, hide yourself in your bedroom and never come out. But don't worry. If you move, I'll come visit loads. So much you'll be inventing new ways to get rid of me."

"Never. I'll never want to get rid of you," she said emphatically.

Saying goodbye to Angeline with a promise to call her with an update, Aylin realized she could not live without Simon and needed to make an attempt to be with him. Even if it ended in heartache for her.

36

"What are you doing sitting behind a desk working instead of going after Aylin?"

"Oliver, so nice of you to barge into my office while I'm trying to work. Do you bloody need something?" he asked testily, gritting his teeth together.

Simon was doing his best to ignore how much he needed Aylin and working twenty-four seven was the only way he could manage it. He came to work early this morning as soon as he woke up. Not even stopping to make breakfast before he left. The dining room had a sandwich delivered to his office for lunch. With Oliver showing up, it reminded him he barely touched it, as it sat half eaten on the edge of his desk.

"Only to tell you you're being an arse. Don't you know what you'll be giving up if you don't go work this shit out with her?"

"I know exactly what I'll be giving up, but I can't be with someone, become too attached and then be happy with it after she leaves to go back home. Let it alone, Oliver. I know what I'm doing," he said with a sigh.

Oliver left and Simon thought he was in the clear, when

Noah and Luke show up at his office door with grim looks on their identical faces.

"What do you two want?" He was tired of being polite. But he would let them talk as long as they left as quickly as possible. Glancing at his paperwork, he pretended to work. Maybe if he didn't pay any attention to them, it would move them along.

"Well, that's not a nice way to greet your favorite cousins," Luke said as he and Noah moved into the room and sat down in the chairs in front of his desk.

"Just say what you want, then get out. I'm busy."

"Aren't you going to ask about how Aylin is doing?" asked Noah.

"Or how the investigation is going?" Luke drawled.

"No, and no." He didn't have the heart for this. Why couldn't they just leave him alone and understand he couldn't keep having Aylin shoved in his face? She was leaving soon...maybe sooner than she planned after her attack. He had to distance himself from her. "If there's nothing else, you know where the door is."

"He has it worse than we thought," Luke mused.

"Yeah, I hope it's not terminal," Noah remarked.

Simon looked up at them. His face screwed up in anger, lips pressed into a flat line, eyes beaded on them. "Get out!" he yelled.

"Sure, after we tell you that Aylin's doing much better. She's progressing so well that we don't need to have someone stay with her all day anymore."

"Of course, that means she's not as protected anymore either," Luke added.

Even with Simon's glare, they continued.

"We told her she should come talk to you, clear up this misunderstanding and move on." Noah blindsided him. Why would he do that? And what misunderstanding? He clearly heard her say it was only a summer fling with him. He couldn't get himself in deeper with her, if she didn't think what they had was more than a fling.

"And she would be safer if you were in her cabin with her at night."

"So what you're saying is that you want me to sleep with her to keep her safe? You both pimps now?" Simon sneered at them. How dare they try to pawn her off on him? It wasn't only insulting to him, but it was downright demeaning toward Aylin.

"Look. We don't have any more information about who attacked Aylin. If you were watching out for her, then we would feel better about her being on her own, while still recovering from her injuries," explained Luke.

Noah continued the conversation. "She's healed enough to no longer need people around her all the time, but we think having all those people with her was precisely why she was safe. We don't know what will happen now that she doesn't need us as much anymore."

"Just think about it." Luke and Noah stood up and walked toward the door. Noah went through and started down the hallway.

"And stop acting like an asshole," Luke called out over his shoulder as he left the room.

As if they were experts about relationships and love. Neither one of them had a steady girlfriend in a long time.

Simon dropped the paper in his hand and felt a twinge of panic. Love? Where did that come from? He barely knew Aylin enough to be in love with her. No, he could not be in love with her.

Lust. Yes, it was just lust. Sure he missed spending time with her. He loved sleeping with her. That was all it was. He let out a deep breath before picking up the paper he was reading again. He'd have to think about that as well.

A couple of hours later, Marinda and Ryleigh stopped by to

start in on him. He'd gotten a little more work done, but no where near what he usually accomplished in a day. His mind kept on wandering to what Luke and Noah told him earlier. What if she wasn't safe in her cabin now that everyone stopped staying with her? Would he be able to live with himself if something else happened to her?

Katia and Hailee stopped by after dinner. Or he thought it was after dinner. Katia was holding a plate of something that smelled delicious. His stomach growled, and he remembered he hadn't eaten all his lunch. His sandwich from lunch was still sitting on the corner of his desk, looking sad and crusty.

"No food until we finish talking to you," Katia said, holding the plate hostage from him.

"Fine, get it over with then," he said, his shoulders slumping in defeat.

"You didn't hear all of Aylin's conversation. She doesn't think all you have is a fling," Hailee told him. She didn't think what they had was only a fling? Could he have been wrong about what he heard? According to Katia and Hailee, he was terribly wrong.

Shit! It was all his fault. If he had just stayed at the cabin and asked her about what he heard, she wouldn't have been out in the woods by herself and attacked. They would have been out to dinner together.

"Aylin loves you. Everyone can tell. But she's afraid. It would be her entire life changing for you, Simon," Katia said.

After they left and he finished the food they brought him, Simon logged off his computer and plugged it in. Putting away the paperwork for another day, he left the office and headed to his apartment. He needed to think about everything he was told today. Maybe he really did get it wrong, and he still had a chance to make it right with Aylin. Would she really stay for him?

Once in his apartment, he changed out of his work clothes

and into a pair of gray sweatpants and a black t-shirt. Both of which had seen better days. Grabbing a beer out of his fridge, he plopped down onto his couch and stared at the blank screen of the tv.

Simon couldn't wrap his head around what he wanted—a life with Aylin. And what he thought he needed—an uncomplicated life without the fear of losing someone he loved.

But isn't that what you are doing by keeping Aylin away, losing someone you love?

At the knock at his door, Simon put his beer down on the coffee table and got up to answer it, surprised to find his father. He actually hadn't thought about him in a while and found another spurt of guilt hit him.

"Hi, Dad. Come on in." Standing off to the side of the door to let his father walk in, he added, "I was just having a beer. Would you like one?"

"No thanks. I wanted to come talk to you." They walked over to his couch and sat down.

"So what's up? Anything wrong? Do you need anything? I know I haven't been coming to see you lately."

His father held up a hand to stop him. "I don't need anything and nothing is wrong. I came by to apologize for causing trouble around the resort."

"You haven't been causing trouble. Dad, you lost Mum and needed something to keep yourself busy. I'm starting to realize why myself."

"I have been causing trouble. But that stops now. I would like to continue working in the job you set up for me and help where ever else I'm needed, but this is your resort. It's not mine anymore and I can't keep on pretending it is. You're doing a wonderful job."

"Thanks, Dad. You know this resort is as much yours as the

rest of us. We'll be happy to have you here in any way you want."

"The other reason I stopped by was to find out what is going on with you."

"Nothing is going on with me. Everything is good." His father stared at him until he looked away. "Okay, it's not going good. I screwed up with Aylin and I miss her."

"Simon, you need to live life, even if that means losing her in the future. You can't put a price on all the good times you'll have in the meantime. If you love Aylin, then you need to grab on and enjoy whatever time you have with her. I realized that talking about all the good times with your mother helped me more than anything else in this world. I will live the rest of my life for her and, most importantly, for myself. Don't go through life missing out on a moment of time with the love of your life."

They spoke for a little longer, he and his father reminiscing about some of the good times with his mother. It was healing to talk about her without worrying his father would be too sad.

After his father left, Simon thought back about all the good times he had with Aylin, and then about everything his family had said to him. He couldn't live without Aylin and needed to go make it work with her. And he loved her too much to make her think he didn't want her with him forever. Hopefully, he would make things right with her.

Looking at his watch, Simon decided it wasn't too late to go to her. He left his apartment to go find Aylin in her cabin.

Back at the sheriff's office, Luke sat at his desk doing his own paperwork when his phone rang. Looking at the readout on his phone, he discovered it was the one person he was waiting on about the extra background checks on Aylin's cabin neighbors.

"Harry, tell me what you've got." Luke listened to the information Harry gave him.

The more he heard, the more he became concerned about Aylin than ever before. The information was not what he had expected, and yet it made so much sense now.

"Thanks, Harry. Yeah, I'll let you know." Hanging up, he needed to rush to the cabin and Aylin as soon as possible.

Her life may depend on it.

37

"Deanna! Oh, you startled me! I was just on my way out." Aylin had opened the door of her cabin to go to Simon, surprised to find her cabin neighbor, Deanna, standing on her doorstep.

She thought she wouldn't need to deal with her neighbor much after Marinda had told Deanna she no longer needed any help and to go enjoy the rest of her vacation. Apparently, she didn't get the hint.

"If you'll excuse me, I'm late meeting someone." She moved forward, trying to influence Deanna into moving back so she could step outside and close the door.

Instead, Deanna caught Aylin off guard and shoved her inside, closing the door before she even had a moment to register what happened. "What are you doing?" This wasn't even remotely funny anymore. How dare she push her into the cabin!

"Shut up and go into the kitchen, bitch." Deanna shoved her again, making her stumble a little over the corner of the rug.

"Now listen here. If you think you can come into my cabin, push me around and call me a bitch, then you don't know who you're dealing with. Get your ass out of my cab—" It was then as she turned toward Deanna that Aylin noticed the gun, stopping her in her tracks.

The woman had a gun and was pointing it right at her! She had a healthy respect for guns and used them frequently in her books. Part of her research required her to take not only a gun safety class, but to spend time in a shooting range trying out various types of weapons. She even spoke to a weapons expert she met at a gun show to learn all about the damage each type of weapon would create when used on a person.

So seeing Deanna pointing a gun directly at her terrified her. Add in that it appeared her neighbor was unstable and Aylin was surprised she could think at all.

Perhaps she should try a different tactic. She heard that repeating the person's name over and over could help.

"Hey, Deanna. What's this all about? There's no need to point a gun at me, Deanna. Let's go sit down and talk about it. Just put down the gun, Deanna, and we can go sit on the sofa and you can tell me what's going on."

"Shut up! I'm sick and tired of listening to you. You ruined my life and now you are going to do what I want you to do!" Deanna waved the gun around as she spoke.

Aylin froze. Okay, that didn't work so well. Keeping her eyes on the gun, she scanned around the cabin through her periphery, looking for a way out or a place she would be safe if the gun went off. Discouraged when she didn't discover a safe place. The only option was to find a way out.

Maybe trying another tactic—repeating what she said— would help defuse her anger. It may work.

"So what you're saying is I ruined your life. How did I do that? I never even met you before you came to stay at the cabin next door," she said, a little snarky. Alright, so no one ever said she was good at talking calmly to someone with a gun pointed at her. Not that she'd ever experienced it before.

Deanna growled at her, grabbed her arm, and started

dragging her to the kitchen table, pushing the gun into her side. Dragging out a chair with her foot, Deanna shoved her onto the chair. Aylin instinctively stood up. The gun pointed right at her head, encouraged her to sit right back down.

As her neighbor pointed the gun right at her head, the door to the cabin opened and her other cabin neighbor, Chris Foster, entered. "It's about time you got here. Tie her up," Deanna ordered.

Chris moved toward Aylin with a hank of rope looped around his arm. She couldn't let him tie her up, but she didn't know how she was going to get out of this, either. If it wasn't for the gun, she could have taken Deanna down earlier.

The woman was slight, and Aylin imagined a strong wind would blow her over. She was about half a foot shorter than her own 5'6" and she couldn't weigh more than a hundred pounds. But now there were two of them and only one of her—the crazy woman had a gun and the behemoth man outweighed her by at least a hundred and fifty pounds.

Aylin had to admit that it didn't look good. Her only hope was if someone decided she needed to be checked on tonight. Not likely, though. No one had been staying the night with her for a couple of days now.

"You should think about this, guys. Kidnapping is a serious charge. If you leave now, we can forget it ever happened."

"Shut her up, Chris." After tying her to the chair, he pulled out a rag—stained with who knew what—from his back pocket and a roll of duct tape.

"No, wait. You don't need that. I—" Chris cut her off by shoving the rag into her mouth. She gagged a little when it touched the back of her throat and tasted like stale grease. Breathing through her nose helped stave off the feeling of wanting to vomit. Breaking off a piece of the tape, he placed it over her mouth.

She was now tied to the chair with a rope wrapped around

her body and weaved around the rungs of the chair, ending with the rope tied around her wrists behind her back. With her mouth full of the rag, she could not use her tongue to work the duct tape off. Aylin was more scared than ever before. Done with his task, he moved over to the front door as though he were on guard.

"I've got you now," Deanna started, waving the hand with the gun around as she spoke. "You didn't think that coming down to Florida would stop me from getting justice for all you've done, did you? Oh, I knew where you were the whole time. You couldn't hide from me."

Aylin's eyes widened. What the hell was she talking about? Was Deanna her stalker?

"If that nosy neighbor of yours didn't call the cops, I would have taken care of you in your apartment when you came home. You were supposed to be in your apartment writing, alone and not paying attention to anyone breaking in and sneaking up on you. I would have made you pay for everything you've done to me."

Oh my god! She was my stalker! This whole time, Aylin and the police thought it was a man stalking her, but it was really Deanna Irwin.

Suddenly, there was a knock at the door. Chris jumped, but remained quiet when Deanna put her finger in front of her mouth. Aylin saw this as her chance to alert someone and tried to make as much noise as possible from behind the gag.

The person knocked again and called out. "Aylin, are you in there? It's Simon. Can we talk?"

Aylin continued to try to alert him, but Deanna came over, putting her hand over her mouth and pinching her nose so she couldn't breathe. "Not one sound or I'll make sure you can't talk ever again. Hear me?" she threatened quietly.

Eyes wide in fear and about to run out of breath, Aylin nodded as much as she was able, with Deanna's hand over her face. Deanna removed her hand, but wrapped it around her forehead, pressing the gun to her head as she listened to Simon leave.

"Chris, dear, go follow him and make sure he doesn't come back. When you're done, you can go back to your cabin. I'll be there as soon as I'm done with her."

"Do you want me to hurt him?" he asked, cracking his knuckles.

"Do whatever you want. I don't care," she growled. At that, Chris opened the door and left the cabin, closing the door behind him. Releasing Aylin, she moved over to the door and re-locked it. "We wouldn't want anyone to disturb us," she said with a smirk.

"Chris is so easy to control. The poor man is so hard up for female attention, it's ridiculous. If only he was smart enough to make sure his job was done right. I convinced him you were a danger to us both—that you would write about him and expose what he's here hiding from.

"He was supposed to get rid of you. Chris was the one who hit you in the woods at my command. The idiot didn't stay to finish the job though—he should have made sure you were dead! He'll probably bungle taking care of Mr. Kerrigan, too. But no worries. There isn't anything he can do to prove it was me. He'll just think it was Chris Foster all along.

"And I'll take care of Chris after I finish with you. A little accident maybe. Or he'll be so distraught when I tell him I found you've been talking to the police about him that he takes his own life. Shoots himself right in his cabin. Won't that be a shame," she said, putting on a fake pout.

Aylin's eyes widened at the scope of how far Deanna was willing to go. "As for you, I'm going to make you pay for ruining my life. No one gets to write about me and my parents the way you did and gets away with it."

This was about one of her books? Aylin didn't remember

ever writing about Deanna or her parents. Then again, she didn't actually write true crime—she wrote crime fiction. She occasionally got ideas from actual news stories, but she couldn't think of any that mentioned Deanna. She didn't know her parents, either. Damn, she was really, truly insane!

"You can't get away with spying on me and my parents. How long have you watched us? My entire life? You won't get away with it any more. Once I'm done with you, my life will be off limits to you and your books!"

She was absolutely certifiable! The thought that she would spy on people to write her books was ridiculous. And what was this about spying on her for her entire life? Deanna couldn't be much more than a year or two younger than she was. The woman had Aylin spying on her from the time she was a toddler. Unbelievable!

And now she was not only worried about herself, but about Simon, too. What was Chris going to do to him? Was he going to be hurt because of her stalker? She had to find a way to get out of this. Aylin wiggled her hands, trying to loosen up the ropes. Damn it! They were too tight and moving her hands around only made them tighter.

Deanna was going on and on about how Aylin destroyed her family through her books, apparently relating every single one to her own life. She didn't know how much more time she had before this crazy woman decided to shoot her.

Feeling deflated, she hoped Simon was alright and would realize something was wrong and call for help.

38

Simon got to Aylin's cabin and knocked on the door, waiting for a response. He knew she was in there. She hadn't left her cabin in weeks, except for doctor appointments and some physical therapy. Though recently she didn't leave for even that. Noah had commandeered one of the stationary bikes from the resort a while after Aylin returned from the hospital.

When Aylin didn't answer, Simon knocked again. "Aylin, are you in there? It's Simon. Can we talk?"

Simon heard nothing coming from inside, and it made him concerned. The lights were on, so she was awake, but it was eerily quiet. Did she fall or have a medical setback? Or was she ignoring him? It was most likely the latter.

He remembered Noah mentioned he was going to hang out at the resort's tavern with Oliver tonight. He'd go back to the resort to ask Noah to check on her. She'd answer the door for him. He would tag along and follow Noah inside, then convince her to listen to him.

As he walked back down the path, he was startled to hear the door of the cabin open behind him. Turning, he hoped to

206

see Aylin. Instead, it shocked him to find someone who should not be coming out of her cabin.

Chris Foster.

What was he doing in her cabin? And why wouldn't they answer when he knocked?

Chris picked up a branch as big around as Luke's forearm that was sitting up against the side of the cabin and walked in his direction instead of toward his own cabin. Simon realized something was not right and fell further into the shadows of the surrounding woods. Was he following him? And more importantly, was Aylin alright?

Not wanting to alert Chris, Simon silenced his phone and opted to text Luke instead of calling him.

> Simon: Need help at Aylin's cabin. Come quick. She's not answering the door. Chris Foster came out of her cabin to follow me. He's heading toward the resort. I'm going to her cabin.

Putting his phone away, he had to get back to the cabin and make sure Aylin was safe. Waiting until Chris had passed by and was far enough to no longer give himself away, Simon stepped back onto the path and walked the short distance to the cabin.

He wasn't sure how to approach this. There were several reasons why Chris was in her cabin. He couldn't think of any of them that were good.

Aylin could have let him in, and after talking to her, he left. That one made little sense to him because Aylin always said he gave her the creeps whenever he was around. Besides, it still didn't explain why she didn't answer her door when he knocked.

Another possibility was that he forced his way inside and hurt her. She could be injured, lying on the floor right now. In that case, Simon should use his key to the cabin—assuming it was locked—and go in through the front door. He needed to get to her as soon as possible. If only the key wasn't still back in his office.

The last option was that Chris didn't go into the cabin alone. If someone else was in the cabin with Aylin, bursting into the cabin would not be wise. She'd get hurt before he'd be able to size up the situation. He did not want to be responsible for her getting hurt.

The curtains covered the view through the front windows of the cabin, and the lights were only shining around the edges. There was no telling if anyone else was with her.

He also had to consider that Chris may come back to the cabin when he didn't find him. Standing in front of the cabin made him a target. He quietly walked around the side of the cabin. At the back of the cabin, he peeked through the bedroom windows, which thankfully had the curtains drawn open.

The room was dark, the moonlight shining behind him illuminated part of the room enough for him to see it was empty. With the door from the bedroom to the living area closed, he couldn't get a good look into the living room.

Continuing to walk down the length of the cabin to the glass patio doors, Simon was relieved to see no one had closed the blinds. He would have a clear view into the cabin, but that also meant whoever was inside could see him, too.

Peeking at the edge of the glass doors without exposing himself to those inside, Simon became alarmed when he found Aylin tied up, gagged, and being held at gunpoint. The bigger surprise was Deanna Irwin, holding the gun.

Did Chris dupe her into watching Aylin for him? Her back turned to him, so he felt comfortable to observe for a little longer. Aylin looked terrified. Her eyes were wide, tears pooling and spilling down her cheeks.

It killed him to see her in this position. Like she hadn't been through so much already. It solidified the fact that he loved her and would do anything and everything possible to have her in his life permanently.

The more Simon watched what was happening in front of him, the more he realized the possibility that it wasn't Chris who was the instigator. It was Deanna. She looked entirely too comfortable with the gun. She became more and more emphatic as she spoke, waving the gun around, almost as if she forgot she was holding it.

He did not want to wait until Luke arrived to help Aylin, but he also didn't know how much longer she had before Deanna did something drastic. Simon had to do something to move Deanna's attention off Aylin and onto him.

But what could he do? Getting her to notice him may only make it worse for Aylin instead of better. Bloody hell! He needed Luke there now. Pulling out his phone, Simon checked to see if his cousin had texted him back.

Nothing. Without knowing if Luke got his message or not, the only other choice he felt he had was to distract Deanna.

He glanced inside once more, this time making eye contact with Aylin. She shook her head slightly, but he couldn't be deterred.

Looking around, the small table and chairs on the patio were about all he had to use. Unless he went back to the front and grabbed a potted plant. Not wanting to risk being seen by Chris Foster, a chair was his best option.

Quietly picking up one of them up, Simon prepared to smash it through the glass door when a loud bang, then another sent the glass careening toward him.

Falling to the ground, the chair lying by his side, he only hoped Aylin was okay and Luke would show up soon.

<h1 style="text-align:center">39</h1>

Aylin saw Simon peeking through the glass doors and was worried Deanna would see him, too. She was so thankful that he was alive after Chris went after him, but she didn't want him to get hurt by being too close to the cabin, either. Deanna would kill him if she thought Simon was getting in her way to make Aylin pay for her so-called spying.

She was worried he would try something on his own and Deanna would shoot him. If he was killed trying to help her, she'd never forgive herself. And she would mourn him for the rest of her life. She loved him so much and didn't know how she would live without him.

Knowing Simon as she did, she was sure he called Luke as soon as he realized something was wrong. But she didn't see Luke. And that meant Simon would try to save her on his own. Aylin had to distract Deanna to give Luke time to arrive. But what could she do all tied up to a chair and gagged with a cloth in her mouth?

"I'm going to make you wish for death by the time I'm done with you," Deanna said. Could she get any more cliché?

It was hard for Aylin to reconcile her emotions. She was

terrified and couldn't keep her body from trembling or the tears from flowing. She didn't want to be shot. Or die. Other than the most recent events of being stalked, she loved her life and didn't want it to end. She wanted to experience what it would be like to share her life with Simon and what the future would bring.

But she also had the urge to roll her eyes at the absurdity coming out of Deanna's mouth. The thought that she would have been spying on Deanna and her parents for her entire life topped them all. Though the way she was still talking, more ridiculous sayings may come out of her mouth before she was done.

"My original plan was to kill you quickly. Surprise you in your apartment and shoot you in the head before you even knew I was there. That would have been sweet karma. You at your computer, writing about my life as if you know anything about it, then BAM! A hole in your head as you slump over your treachery. But no! You weren't fucking there!" Deanna screamed at her.

"You ruined my plans. So I left you a message before your nosy neighbor called the police and interrupted me. Then you had to fucking leave! You were supposed to be too frightened to leave your damn apartment. I was going to wait until you were sleeping, climb through your fire escape window and stab you in your traitorous heart. You. Were. Not. There! It took me a lot of time and money to find you down here in Florida. To make up for all my trouble, bitch, I'm going to kill you slowly. After everything you put me through, I need something to make me happy."

Aylin was horrified to realize how close she came to being killed in her apartment in Philadelphia. Deanna was getting more and more unhinged as she was speaking, continuing to flail the gun around as she spoke.

Her hair, usually neatly styled in an updo, was coming apart around her face and neck. Her face was red with anger and if how she was looking at her could kill her outright, Aylin would have died ten times over by now.

Glancing over at the glass doors, she finally made eye contact with Simon. Shaking her head, she hoped to discourage him from making a scene that would direct Deanna's attention to him. Instead, he picked up one of the patio chairs, just knowing he was about to break the glass. She couldn't let him do that. It was too dangerous without having Luke to back him up. Simon didn't have any weapons, and she didn't want to see what would happen if he entered the cabin to help.

A scream told her Deanna noticed him. Running behind Aylin, she grabbed her around the neck, shooting at Simon through the glass doors. Bang, bang! Two shots in quick succession.

Aylin let out a muffled scream from behind her gag as she watched Simon fall to the ground. Was he hit? Was he safe? Was he still alive? She would give anything to know what was happening with him right now.

Holding the gun to her head, Deanna started screaming. "I will kill you all. You have no idea the danger you put yourself in by coming here, Mr. Kerrigan," she sneered.

Leaning down, she harshly whispered in Aylin's ear. "What do you think? Is he lying there bleeding out? Have you ever seen what happens when someone is shot? It's marvelous when you shoot them in just the right spot. You can practically see the blood pump out in time to their heart beating. It really is quite mesmerizing. Maybe I should go check on how your dear Mr. Kerrigan is doing. Make sure he's really dead. We wouldn't want any witnesses."

Aylin saw the bottom half of Simon's legs. He wasn't moving, and she was afraid she had lost him. She came so close to finally finding the one person who made her feel alive. Like she wanted to do more than close herself up in a room and write all day. And now it may be all over before they really got to begin. He could be lying there bleeding out or dead.

If he was dead, then she didn't want to think about how her life would be without him. But she also wasn't about to just sit all tied up and not try to help. She needed to do something to slow Deanna down before she went over to Simon.

If he was still alive, he needed more time for someone else to come find him. There was no way he would have come to save her without contacting his cousin first. Luke had to be on the way and right now she was the only one who could buy Simon some time until he arrived.

Deanna released her neck, removing the gun from against her head, as she prepared to walk around Aylin to go toward the smashed glass doors to check on Simon. Going over every scenario in her head, she had to be quick. She also knew it may mean getting shot herself. It was a risk she had to take to save him.

Gripping the slats of the chair behind her, she gained more leverage. As Deanna walked around her, she sprung up and made a running sweep across the woman's arm and waist.

Catching her by surprise, she knocked her down to the ground; the gun skittering across the floor toward the kitchen island, stopping under a stool. Not being able to stop her momentum, Aylin fell heavily on Deanna, knocking the wind out of herself.

It wasn't as easy as she had hoped. Being tied to the chair didn't allow her to stand up straight when she rushed the woman, nor was she able to control how she would land once she hit her. She was uncomfortably lying on top of Deanna, who was squirming and trying to move out from under her. Aylin couldn't let that happen, so she relaxed as much as possible and let the weight of her body and the chair compress Deanna further into the floor.

"Get off me, you stupid bitch! You've ruined my life! I. Will. Kill. You."

"Well, that's quite a confession. I must say, you're making my job a lot easier."

Turning her head, she saw Luke standing in the blown out doorway with a couple of his deputies behind him. "Take care of her," he said, pointing his deputies toward Deanna. "I'll take care of Ms. Miller."

Luke carefully lifted her upright, as his deputies struggle to contain Deanna. Carefully removing the tape from over her mouth, he helped her take out the rag. Her mouth, tongue, and throat felt dry, making it hard to talk. "Simon," she croaked out.

"Noah has him."

"Was he shot?"

"No, but some of the flying glass hit him. He'll be fine once Noah stitches him up."

She slumped in relief to know Simon wasn't shot. Luke untied her hands and unwind the rope from around her and the chair as they watched his deputies cuff Deanna. The woman was still struggling with them, cursing that she was the victim and they were all going to pay for it. The words becoming fainter as they led her outside.

With the rope removed, Aylin moved her arms after what felt like days, but was really only a couple of hours. The blood rushed to her hands and fingers, causing little pinpricks of pain. Her arms felt stiff, her joints aching and her muscles tight. Rubbing her wrists where the rope dug in, she followed beside Luke, where he guided her to the couch, his arm around her waist.

"What happened?" Luke inquired once she was sitting. He took a seat in the chair opposite the couch, waiting for her to answer. Before she could talk, Simon barreled in, Noah right behind him.

40

"Where is she? Is she alright?" Simon asked in a panicked tone.

"Simon, you need to let me get that glass out," Noah insisted.

He didn't want to hear it. He needed to make sure Aylin wasn't hurt. Just the thought of her being hurt again made him feel like his entire world was collapsing around him. He heard the crash and Deanna screaming right before Luke went into the cabin, but he could not see what was going on. Noah had prevented him from getting up, saying he needed to stay where he was until he made sure Simon's injuries weren't severe and Luke gave the all clear.

Screw that! As soon as it was over, he was up and moving inside the cabin, his shoes crunching on broken glass. He wasn't about to admit how hard it was to get up or how he hurt all over.

"I'm fine, Simon," Aylin insisted. She looked alright. She was rubbing her hands over her wrists, trying to increase the circulation back, he supposed. But other than that and red-rimmed eyes, she looked fine. Most likely better than he looked at the moment.

"Now that you know Aylin is fine, sit down so I can check out your injuries." Noah guided him by the arm to a table chair.

"Just check Aylin first. It sounded like she fell and you know she's still recovering from her head injury. I promise I'll go sit down and you can take care of me after."

Noah reluctantly let go of his arm and walked over to Aylin. After doing a quick check-up, he declared she had a few more bumps, scrapes, and bruises, but was otherwise doing well. He walked back over to Simon and had him carefully remove his shirt, which was ripped and bloody.

"You're lucky you didn't get shot. Some of these cuts are deep, though, and it'll take some time to remove the glass before I can sew them up. We really should go to the clinic."

"No. I want to stay here." Simon wasn't about to leave now that he was here with Aylin. And he wanted to hear what Luke had to say about what happened.

"Alright, but I don't recommend it. If I miss any small pieces of glass and stitch you up, it could delay the healing process and cause an infection."

"You just let me worry about that, Noah." Noah wasn't pleased, but Simon wasn't concerned. Still, his cousin walked over to the kitchen to grab a small bowl, returning with it before pulling out small shards of glass with tweezers and plopping the glass into the bowl.

While Noah took care of him, Luke laid out what he learned. "I was actually coming here already before Simon texted me. I received a call about the check I requested from some friends of mine on your cabin neighbors."

"Oh my gosh, I forgot about Chris Foster! He—" Aylin began.

Luke interrupted. "Don't worry about Chris. I have someone picking him up as we speak."

Aylin let out a breath and Simon admitted he was relieved about it as well.

Pulling out a small notebook from his shirt pocket, Luke continued. "Deanna Irwin's real name is Deanna Hill. She has a long history of drugs and prostitution, starting when she was a child. Her parents were known for distribution and use of drugs, and throwing wild parties. Apparently, when Deanna was about five years old, one partygoer took her hostage. Her parents fled, leaving her when the police showed up. That was the first time she was removed from the home. She was in and out of the foster care system. By the time she was eight, there was a report of her stabbing another child in her foster home. She was arrested and placed in juvenile detention. Eventually, her parents somehow got her back when she was twelve. They started having her run drugs for them and it was the first time she started using them, too. Mostly, she managed to do this and still go to school. Most likely to keep child protective services from taking her again." Luke paused for a moment, flipping the page before continuing.

"When she was fifteen, her parents included her in their latest drug deal."

"They sold her," Aylin said flatly.

"Yes, they started prostituting out their daughter. And if my reports are accurate, she didn't object in the long term. When she was eighteen, Deanna left her parents for good. She remained off the radar for a few years, though we suspect she was still using drugs—sometimes selling them—and selling her body for some extra cash. She was never caught. About a year ago, Deanna Irwin was born. It was the first time she existed with that name."

"And right after that, I had a stalker," Aylin concluded. "Hey, how do you know so much about her childhood? Isn't that stuff sealed?"

Luke smirked. "I have my ways."

Obviously, there was more to the time Luke spent in the

military than they knew. Simon wondered about that and thought they would need to have a conversation about it soon.

"After she stopped using Deanna Hill, it was like she disappeared. Plenty of information on her parents. They were arrested over and over for drug distribution and running a prostitution ring. Her father died in jail. Nasty business. Someone didn't like how he prostituted young girls. The mother died a few years ago, but reports show it wasn't natural or from her own hand. Apparently, someone gave her enough drugs to kill a man twice her size. Police closed it out as an overdose."

"What about Chris Foster?" Simon asked, wincing when Noah hit a sensitive spot while removing another piece of glass. With as much information as Luke had on Deanna, he most likely had the same on Chris.

"Yes, well, as I said before, Chris is local. Not to Cypress Bay anyway, but from a few counties over. So not my jurisdiction. The story was he came here on vacation to do some fishing and relax for the summer. He rented the cabin to escape from being arrested again after beating his wife up for trying to kick him out for cheating on her. She pressed charges. Few women who suffer through abuse do, but she said he'd done it—the cheating and the beatings—one too many times and she would not take it anymore even if it meant he would kill her. After speaking with her, I have to say she's a very brave woman. She's getting therapy and help to get back on her feet."

"Deanna said he was hiding out here. He's the one who hit me in the woods. He was supposed to kill me, but Deanna said he messed it up. She was going to tell him I talked to the police about him—that I found out why he was here. She was going to kill him and make it look like he did it himself," Aylin explained.

"He wouldn't have been able to hide for too long. He wasn't that bright and registered for the cabin in his own name. It was only a matter of time before we picked him up," Luke responded.

Simon tuned out the rest of the conversation. It hit him he could have lost Aylin for good that day in the woods. If Chris had made sure she was dead, he never would have had the chance to find her. She would have been dead, lying in the woods.

And he never would have had more time with her—the kind of life he was always wishing for. A wife and children. Someone who was there for him. This was what his father was trying to tell him. He couldn't control what happened in life. People got hurt, people died. But it's the time in between—the love and joy and times spent together—that mattered the most.

41

The sun streamed through the window blinds the next morning as Aylin woke up sore but happy to be alive and in relatively one piece. She supposed it was nice to wake up to a bright sunny day after everything she experienced. Luke and Noah dragged Simon out of the cabin when she said she needed to have some time for herself for the night. He left reluctantly once she promised they would talk the next day.

After everyone left, she took a bath and soaked in it for an hour, emptying and refilling the water several times to keep the temperature just this side of scalding. It helped her body feel better, but did little to calm her down on the inside. On the inside, she was a mess of emotions.

Aylin couldn't believe everything that had happened. She was kidnapped, tied up, gagged, and had a gun pointed at her. She found out the small, diminutive woman in the next cabin was her stalker at home. That same woman used the man, who seriously gave her the creeps, in the other cabin next to her to kill her. And the things Luke said about them both. She felt so lucky to be alive.

Sleep came in fits last night, but Aylin felt more at peace

now that her stalkers were arrested. Stalkers, plural, because Chris Foster was just as much a stalker as Deanna Irwin, um, Hill. She had sympathy for Deanna as a child, yet none for her as an adult. She made her own choices after leaving her parents. Chris was just plain scary, and he always gave her the creeps.

Now that they were both out of her life—hopefully for good—she had to figure out what she wanted to do with her life. Did she want to go back home to Philadelphia? Her apartment, Angeline, and parents were all waiting for her. But what else would she have other than what it always was?

Her life back home wasn't bad—far from it—yet she admitted now that it was a lonely life. She spent most of her time cloistered away in her apartment. If it wasn't for Angeline, she would never leave it.

Aylin didn't realize what she was missing until she came down to Cypress Bay. Here she worked, just as she did at home. But the Kerrigans didn't let her shut herself away for long. Someone always seemed to know when she needed to go out for lunch or dinner or just to have some time with other people.

And then there was Simon. She loved him. So much. Last night almost killed her more than Deanna wanted. To witness him lying on the ground after that bitch shot at him. She thought he was dead or dying. Aylin didn't know what she would have done if he had died. Especially with their relationship undefined up to that point. If she had lost him at that moment, she would never have known whether they could have made it work, or if he even wanted them to try.

But now...now she had another chance. She was on her way to go talk to him when Deanna caught her at the cabin door. She wouldn't leave to go back home until she spoke with him.

They had some sort of connection. Call it lust or whatever. They wouldn't have spent so much time together in and out of bed without lust and, for her, respect for him as a person. What she didn't know was if he loved her.

Aylin couldn't stay with him for anything less than love. She loved him so much that she would let him go if he didn't love her in return.

Getting out of bed, she took care of her morning routine in the bathroom and came out to dress in her room. She wouldn't dress up for him. Aylin was someone who was more comfortable in jeans. She liked pretty shirts, so she put on one in a color and cut that favored her, a muted blue and form fitting short-sleeve shirt with a v-neck. And she often kept her hair up in a ponytail to keep it out of her face while she worked. It was who she was and if Simon didn't love, or even like, her for who she was, then he wasn't the man for her.

She didn't know why she was trying to talk herself out of a relationship with Simon. Of course, he was the man for her! She was confident in the way she felt about him and envisioned the future with him. It was how he felt about her and their future that she was unsure about.

Not wanting to take the time thinking too hard about it and working herself up, the only way to know was to find Simon and talk to him. She wouldn't even stop for breakfast first. This was too important and could change her whole life for the better. Walking quickly toward the door, she picked up the key to the cabin and opened the door.

The first thing she saw was Simon walking down the path and through the trees toward her cabin. His head was down and he looked as though he was in deep thought. Enjoying the time to watch him without him knowing, Aylin took in his rumpled appearance of gray sweats and a black t-shirt. His hair mussed like he jumped out of bed and immediately left to come to her. A few areas on his arms were red or stitched from when the flying glass hit him. She felt so thankful it wasn't any worse.

"Simon."

His head lifted quickly at the sound of his name breaking the quiet of the morning. A smile tugged at the corner of his mouth as he walked up to her after letting out a deep breath. "Aylin," he responded.

"Come on, let's go inside and talk." Nodding, Simon followed her inside and moved into the living room while she closed the door.

<h1 style="text-align:center">42</h1>

Watching Aylin close and lock the door, Simon stood in the middle of the living room, waiting for her to come to him. He didn't want to waste any more time without her.

Almost losing Aylin made everything crystal clear to him and now he absolutely knew that it was better to love her for as long as he would be allowed to have her in his life than to never have her in it at all.

Not being able to wait through a conversation before having her in his arms, he reached out to her, cradling her face with both hands. "I need to get this out of the way before we talk." Bending down, he pressed his lips to hers, lightly licking them until she opened to him.

They gently caressed their tongues together like a seductive mating ritual, sipping at each other's lips. Her hands came up to wrap around his forearms to steady herself. The wounds stung, but he didn't care. All he cared about was having her in his arms again.

Slowly pulling back, he whispered, "I missed you," before releasing his hands from her face.

"I missed—oh no! Your stitches!" She released her hands

quickly from around his arms when she noticed where they were resting. "I'm so sorry. Are you alright? Did I hurt you?"

"I'm fine, love. Let's go sit down and talk now." He took her hand in his, threading his fingers around her own, and walked over to the couch. Sitting down, he steadily pulled her down next to him, not releasing his hand from hers.

"Are you sure you're alright? Why don't you have them covered?"

"Noah told me to take the gauze off this morning," Simon told her.

She looked into his eyes. "To finish what I was saying earlier, I missed you, too."

"I know you needed some time last night after what happened. I would have preferred to stay here with you, even if it was to sleep on the couch. But I understand why you wanted me to go. I didn't understand last night. I really gave Luke and Noah a hard time for dragging me out of here." Simon wasn't sure how he was going to make it up to her, but he'd give it everything he had in him to do so. "After everything that happened between the two of us. How I screwed up every time you needed me the most. I—"

Aylin put the fingers of her free hand over his mouth. "You didn't screw anything up. Katia and Hailee told me what happened. We both had a bit of miscommunication, didn't we?"

"I suppose we did. I should have stayed and talked to you about what I heard instead of leaving. And I never should have said what I did to the guys in my office. What you said on the phone hurt me and I was letting it out the only way I knew how. It didn't even cross my mind that you would come by and hear me. I'm so sorry that you did, and that I hurt you in return. If I didn't leave, we would have cleared everything up and gone out to dinner. You wouldn't have been in the woods when Chris attacked you. If I didn't find you when I did..." Simon felt all choked up over what could have happened. Lifting their clasped hands, he nuzzled her hand against his face after giving it a quick kiss.

"You can't think that way, Simon. You can't look back on the past and have regrets about things that already were. The past has already happened and can't be changed. You can only look at what's happening now and look forward to what's possible." She cupped his face with her other hand. "What do you want to see happen, Simon?"

Simon knew what he wanted, but wasn't sure if it was too soon for Aylin.

He wanted her to love him as he loved her and to move in with him.

He wanted her to marry him, to build a family with her they could raise together.

He wanted to know she was in their apartment at the resort writing, while he was in his office or in meetings.

And he wanted to grow old with her, watching their children grow and become whoever they want. He wondered if they would want the resort as he had growing up.

He wanted so much.

"Well, to start, love, I want to know how you feel about staying here in Florida."

"I'm open to that. I can work anywhere. And I guess I'm getting used to the heat down here."

He chuckled. "It's only the beginning of July."

"Don't tell me it gets worse. It's better if I don't know."

"Well, we'll know how you feel about the heat by the end of August, love, but we have air conditioning."

"That's the third time you've called me 'love'."

"It is, huh? That's the second thing. I love you, Aylin," he said, giving her a light kiss.

"I love you, too, Simon." They sat together holding each other, their eyes meeting and saying more than only the words. "Is there a third thing? Not that those first two weren't enough. I'm just curious."

"Yes, there's a third thing. Will you move into the resort apartment with me, Aylin?" he asked. Noticing she was about to reply, he quickly added, "Don't give me an answer yet. I want you to be sure because you're it for me. There will be no one else who I want in my life as much as I want you."

Noticing the tears gather in her eyes, he added with a bit of panic. "Let's have some fun together for the day. Relax, knowing the danger is over. Come to the fireworks display with me tonight. You'll love our 4th of July fireworks over the lake. And it's perfect since you just got your independence back after everything you've been through. Tomorrow is soon enough to answer. And if you're not comfortable living with me yet, I'll help you find a place of your own. You could even stay in the cabin for as long as you want. I only want you to be with me and to give us a chance."

With tears now slipping down her cheeks, she untangled her hands from his, putting them on his shoulders before straddling him. Simon wrapped his arms around her, holding her close. Running one of her hands behind his head and the other on his cheek, she replied. "I don't need any time to think. You're it for me, too. I would love to move in with you, Simon. The sooner, the better. And once we move my stuff from the cabin to your apartment, we can go enjoy the rest of our day and watch the fireworks. Or we could make some fireworks of our own."

And that's exactly what they set out to do.

43

2 months later.

Simon entered their apartment after a shortened day at work. He knew Aylin worked in the spare room they changed into an office. It was the first thing they did after moving her stuff over from the cabin, so she would have a place to write. Her work was important to her, and it was important for him to give her that space rather than have a guest bedroom he never used.

Peeking into the room, he confirmed she was deep into her writing and wouldn't hear him if he tried to talk to her. Knowing they still had over an hour before she needed to be ready for the party they were having this evening, he left her to continue her work in peace.

Walking into their bedroom to shower and change, he thought about what the last months were like after declaring their love for each other and deciding to live together.

The week after the holiday—and that was a marvelous night, fireworks in the sky and with Aylin—he went with her to Philadelphia to pack up her apartment, where she didn't seem to have a hard time deciding what to bring, what to store, and what to donate. They packed up the smaller items, but hired movers to handle the rest.

He loved how no nonsense it was, but with a burst of color here and there. She wryly told him that Angeline declared her impossible with decorating and brought all the color into the apartment little by little until it looked exactly how she thought Aylin's apartment should be styled. He told her they would need her to come down to make sure their apartment at the resort was decorated appropriately then. She readily agreed.

When she introduced him to her friend, he reiterated that thought. Angeline was a bubbly woman who brought even more life to everyone around her. Especially Aylin. She lit up around her friend and was more animated and talkative than she was away from her. He noticed they were more like sisters than best friends, and so he imagined she would stay with them in their guest room frequently. He found he was okay with that.

Later during the trip, she brought him to meet her parents for dinner at her childhood home. He loved them immediately. They were warm and caring people who loved their only child. They were concerned at first about how quickly they were moving in their relationship, but by the end of the night, they seemed to accept they were meant to be together.

Watching her parents together reminded him of them. It was obvious they deeply loved each other. The way Aylin's father looked at her mother and vice versa gave him even more confidence they were right for each other. Because that was how he and Aylin looked at each other.

And if he was honest with himself, it was how his mother and father had looked at each other, too. With love so strong, everyone saw it in every look, touch, and sigh.

Finishing up in the bathroom, he wrapped a towel around his waist and strolled out into their bedroom to the closet.

Grabbing a clean pair of black slacks, a black belt, and a white button-down shirt, he walked to the bed and laid them out before grabbing a pair of underwear from the dresser. Sliding them on, he removed the towel and draped it over a chair.

As he continued dressing, Simon thought he should be more nervous about this party than he was. They were having the party in the ballroom at the Cypress Bay Manor Resort. They often rented out the ballroom for parties, conventions, wedding receptions, and sometimes community events. Tonight it would be for their family and friends to honor and celebrate the life of Simon's mother, Lauren, and Simon and Aylin's new relationship.

His father was finally ready to move forward in his life and wanted to remember all the good times he had with his wife. Simon had Aylin to thank for that, too. She gave his father, John, the space to talk and allowed him to work out his feelings about losing his wife when Aylin was stuck in her cabin recovering.

His family also wanted to celebrate his new relationship with Aylin. They all had a part in helping them work through their miscommunications. What she didn't know was that he also planned to use the gathering as an engagement party.

Pulling out a small velvet box from his nightstand, he opened it up to show a simple ring of sterling silver with a solitaire round sapphire and small diamonds surrounding it. He thought the sapphire suited her auburn hair, blue eyes and recent sun-kissed complexion.

He would ask her to marry him tonight during the party. Everyone knew except for Aylin and were on strict orders to not breathe a word of it. Oliver even made a special cake to bring out after he asked her. Simon had called Angeline and her parents, asking if they could attend. Angeline barely let him get the question out before she was booking a flight to Orlando. Marinda picked her up from the airport this morning and had been keeping her busy and away from Aylin all day.

Her parents could not come down, but asked if someone would send a video of the proposal to them. Angeline was going to take care of that, and brought down an engagement present from Aylin's parents, too. They promised to come visit in another couple of months.

Sliding the ring box into his pants pocket, Simon walked out of the bedroom to make sure Aylin was at a stopping point to prepare for tonight's festivities.

At the door to her office, Simon watched her typing away on her keyboard. He hated having to disturb her while she was in the middle of writing, but knew she didn't want to be late for the party.

"Aylin, it's almost time to go to the party."

Her head shot up. "Huh, what?"

"It's time to get ready for the party, love."

"Oh, right." She saved her work, then stood up, heading for him and the door. "Thank you for reminding me." She leaned up to give him a light kiss before moving to walk around him.

When she was next to him, he wrapped his arm around her waist and pulled her closer to him, giving her a deeper kiss. "Mmmm...now that's better," he said. "Let's go get you ready, love."

"Simon, if you help me get ready, we'll never go to the party," she chuckled.

Smirking at her, Simon knew she was right. He reluctantly let her go, watching her walk to their bedroom to shower and change. While she was, he made a few phone calls to make sure everything and everyone was in place.

Forty-five minutes later, Aylin walked out of the bedroom wearing a blue form-fitted wraparound dress with a deep V in the front. The hemline brushed her knees, showing her fabulous legs that led down to some killer silver shoes. His heart felt like it was going to come out of his chest just looking at her. And he wasn't sure if he was going to make it through the night without wanting to drag her back to their apartment.

He remembered the girls taking her shopping to find a dress for the party, then refusing to show it to him by having it wrapped in a black plastic covering. Apparently, they made sure it matched the ring he bought her, too. Sneaky cousins. She rarely wore dresses, preferring jeans, so it was a real treat for him when she dressed up.

Hand on his heart, Simon looked at her again from head to toe. "You are gorgeous, love. Are you sure we need to go to the party?"

"Thank you. And yes, we need to go to the party. Everyone will be waiting for us."

"Okay. If we must, we must." Sticking his arm out for her, she wrapped her hand around his bicep.

"So I know your father, brother, and cousins will be there, but who else again?"

"Everyone. All my aunts and uncles. My best friend, Joel Madris, is finally back from wherever he went off to. I can't wait until you two can meet."

"He's the one who owns the boat tour company?"

"Yes. Then there will be some other friends of the family, like Sean Cooper, his sister, Emma, and their parents. And our staff here at the resort. They really loved Mum, too. Any of the staff working tonight will rotate in so they can enjoy the party."

"Okay...so a lot of people."

"Don't be nervous. I promise you will have the best night ever."

She smiled up at him. He felt her instantly relax, and he was happy he could do that for her. Just like she did for him.

At the ballroom, they passed the sign informing guests of the private party and walked into the room. Blue and silver decorations filled the room, white table cloths adorned the tables. He really needed to talk to his cousins. If he didn't know better, he would think they were more excited about him proposing to Aylin than he was.

At the right of the room, a line of buffet tables held food, a staff of caterers behind them waiting to serve guests. Simon didn't want his kitchen staff to feel any additional pressure by asking them to make and serve the food, so he hired a catering service, with Oliver in charge of making the food selections. Since food was his speciality, he wouldn't have it any other way. Besides, Oliver said if the food sucked, he would never let anyone else cater a family event again. Simon had chuckled at that. Oliver was a stickler for good food and he was happy his brother wanted to work at the resort with him.

It looked like everyone had arrived, mingling with each other. Simon sought his friend Joel. Seeing him talking with Sean, he walked them in that direction, introducing them to Aylin.

Marinda, Katia, and Ryleigh huddled together, so he caught their eyes and glared at them. They just laughed. Now he knew exactly who was responsible for all the blue and silver.

"Aylin!" At the scream coming from the doorway, Aylin turned to find her friend Angeline.

She was speechless. He stood with a smile on his face, looking down at her. "Go ahead," he said, giving her a little nudge.

She looked at him with tears swimming in her eyes. "Thank you for getting her here."

He watched her walk over to her friend, then embracing each other as though they hadn't seen each other in years instead of a couple of months ago. He knew it felt like years to them, though. They were used to seeing each other every day.

They walked over to Simon and he hugged Angeline, whispering in her ear. "Thank you. She wouldn't want this to happen without you."

"I wouldn't want it to happen without me either," she chuckled, pulling out her phone, stepping back away from them as she tapped away on it. Pointing the phone at them, Simon knew she was taking a video of what was about to come for Aylin's parents.

"Wouldn't want what to happen? The party?" Aylin asked, catching what Angeline said.

"No. This." Facing Aylin, Simon pulled out the velvet box from his pocket, knelt down in front of her, and opened the box to show her the ring inside.

"Blue and silver," she observed, looking around the room and down at her dress, before her eyes came back to the ring.

His eyes lit with humor. "Yeah...I'll need to talk to the girls about that." He could hear the girls giggle behind him. Yes, he would definitely talk to them, he thought.

"Aylin," he began. "For my entire life, all I ever wanted was to find a woman I could love and have a family of my own, like my parents had. When my mother died, I let that dream die with her. I couldn't imagine loving someone that much and then losing her. I saw the pain my father went through and decided it was no longer for me.

"But then you came along. At first, I didn't know what to think or feel. I turned the corner and there was a beautiful woman causing chaos at my resort's front desk. I was still fighting that need of having my own family, but that's all I saw when I looked at you. I was angry at myself for even letting those emotions come through after who we'd just lost. As though there was no room for anything but grief at that moment. Only thoughts of you broke through and before I knew it, you were all I could think about. The only one who was perfect for me. The only one I wanted in my life. And the only one I would ever love. Aylin, please put me out of my misery and agree to be my wife. Create that family with me, love."

Tears were streaming down her face, but her smile was the brightest he had ever seen. "Yes, Simon. I love you so much and I'd love for you to be my husband and make a family with you."

At the surrounding cheers, he took the ring out of the box and, taking her left hand, placed it on her finger. Her arms came around his waist as his hands cradled her face as they kissed, ignoring all the well-wishes and congratulations around them.

EPILOGUE

Oliver Kerrigan watched as Simon and Aylin kissed. He was happy for his brother and he had grown to love Aylin as his own sister. Now she would be his sister-in-law.

Directing one of the catering crew to bring out the cake, Oliver knew this would be the start of the next generation of Kerrigans. He made a bet with Noah, Luke, Sean, and Joel that there would be a baby Kerrigan by this time next year. They took that bet with Joel, saying it would be exactly nine months from today. Glancing back over at Simon and Aylin, he admitted Joel may be right. Well, losing twenty bucks would be well worth it.

"Wasn't that the most romantic proposal ever?"

Oliver looked over his shoulder at the triplets. He knew they purposely went overboard with the blue and silver. As soon as they saw the ring, they bought up every blue and silver decoration they could find. He even got into the act and decorated the engagement cake with silver edible ball bearings and blue flowers.

His cousins were the romantic sort. He wasn't really surprised that Hailee, Katia, and Marinda got involved—that

Ryleigh did, too, was a miracle. She was the more cynical cousin out of all the girls. But she went all in with the decorating, building support frames to drape all the decorations around. There wasn't a single part of the room that didn't have some sort of blue and silver.

Simon was going to scold them. He thought they were brilliant.

"Did you hear that Demi-Lyn is coming back to stay?"

Oliver's whole body tensed up. What did Katia say? No, he could not have heard that Demi-Lyn Shaw was coming back to stay here in Cypress Bay. He had to have been mistaken.

Turning to face them, he had to make sure he heard correctly. "Hey Katia, did you say that Demi-Lyn was coming to Cypress Bay?"

"Hey, Oliver. Yes, she decided to come stay at her parent's lake home."

"Oh," he said casually. "Is she coming down for vacation with her parents? It's been a while since I've seen them at their vacation home."

He actually lived one house away from the Shaw's lake home. He bought it a few years ago when it went up for sale and finished renovating it last year. Oliver always wanted a home on the lake that also gave him a place to get away from work when he wasn't at the resort. Of course, the first thing he renovated in the home was the kitchen. He spent a lot of time coming up with new menus in his spare time and frequently tested out the recipes that went along with them.

"Oh no, you haven't heard! Demi-Lyn's parents died in a car accident. She decided that after she takes care of selling their house in Maryland, she'd keep the lake house and move down here permanently. She doesn't really have any other family in Maryland, anyway."

That was not what he wanted to hear. He was sorry to hear about Demi-Lyn's parents. They had always been nice, and losing them both at once like that would be devastating to her.

Demi-Lyn and Katia became fast friends during the summers her family vacationed in Cypress Bay. So she was always around the lake when he was growing up each summer. She and Katia kept in touch.

In the last few years since he'd bought his lake home, he hadn't seen the Shaws. They didn't come down anymore, and he thought they were only using it as a vacation rental. Apparently, Demi-Lyn would now make it her home. He wasn't sure how to feel about that. Oliver didn't consider them to be friends, though they were friendly toward each other. He much preferred spending time with his male cousins and friends back then.

Yet thinking of Demi-Lyn coming back had him thinking about the last time he saw her. He was seventeen—about to turn eighteen—and was preparing to leave for college that fall. She was fourteen and growing out of her gangly limbs. He knew she had a crush on him. And now he would be practically living next door to her.

Of course, just because she lived one house over, didn't mean he had to spend time with her. They were adults now. Oliver was sure she outgrew her crush. After twelve years, there was no reason to worry about seeing her again.

He'd go about his life as usual. It would be fine. He didn't let things like emotions get the best of him. He was a rock. Solid and unyielding.

Yes, that's what he would be. No problem...bring on Demi-Lyn Shaw.

Curious about how the Kerrigans got started in Cypress Bay? Get an exclusive prequel about John and Marinda Kerrigan, the grandparents of The Kerrigan Family by signing up for my newsletter by either clicking above or going to www.andreafinnelly.com.

***

Thank you for reading Better With You! If you enjoyed it, your recommendations and reviews would be appreciated—they mean so much to indie authors.

***

Want more? Find out what happens between Oliver and Demi-Lyn when she comes back to Cypress Bay in Coming Home To You:

The last time Oliver Kerrigan saw Demi-Lyn Shaw, she was only fourteen years old. Now she's all grown up and back in Cypress Bay.

Unfortunately, someone wants what Demi has and will not stop until he gets it. Will Oliver be able to get his act together before Demi decides it's not safe for her to be back in Cypress Bay for good?

Available October 2025: https://andreafinnelly.com/book/coming-home-to-you/

ABOUT THE AUTHOR

Andrea Finnelly writes both contemporary romantic suspense and paranormal fantasy romance—two genres that let her explore everything from small-town danger to otherworldly magic. Her debut series, The Kerrigan Family, follows eight siblings and cousins as they navigate love and the hazards that pursue them.

Originally from New England, she now lives in the South, where hurricanes and heat waves are wearing out their welcome. When Andrea's not writing, she's watching hockey, auto racing, Doctor Who, home improvement, and paranormal shows. She also loves curling up on her couch to read, and scanning homes for sale in a climate that's cooler and without a lot of snow.

For more books and updates:
www.andreafinnelly.com

ALSO BY ANDREA FINNELLY

The Kerrigan Family Series

Founding Hearts: John & Marinda (Exclusive subscriber prequel)

Better With You: Simon & Aylin

Coming Home To You: Oliver & Demi-Lyn (October 2025)

Always Been You: Noah & Emma (January 2026)

It Had To Be You: Luke & Gracie (April 2026)

Hooked On You: Hailee & Joel (July 2026)

Finding Home With You: Marinda & Sean (October 2026)

Falling For You: Ryleigh & Dillon (January 2027)

Then There Was You: Katia & Beck (April 2027)